Kenny

& the Book of Beasts

written and illustrated by

TONY DiTERLIZZI

Simon & Schuster Books for Young Readers

NEW YORK   LONDON   TORONTO
SYDNEY   NEW DELHI

For NORTON JUSTER,
who I am fortunate to call my friend

Acknowledgments

Tony would like to thank

JUSTIN CHANDA AND THE ENTIRE S&S TEAM;

STEVE BERMAN; BEATRICE CODY AND WILL EBERLE;

ELLEN GOLDSMITH-VEIN; JODI REAMER;

CAROL MALONEY NELSON; EMILY RICH;

SCOTT FISCHER; MY BRILLIANT WIFE, ANGELA;

AND OUR AWESOME DAUGHTER, SOPHIA.

SIMON & SCHUSTER BOOKS FOR YOUNG READERS · An imprint of Simon & Schuster Children's Publishing Division · 1230 Avenue of the Americas, New York, New York 10020 · This book is a work of fiction. Any references to historical events, real people, or real places are used fictitiously. Other names, characters, places, and events are products of the author's imagination, and any resemblance to actual events or places or persons, living or dead, is entirely coincidental. · Copyright © 2020 by Tony DiTerlizzi · All rights reserved, including the right of reproduction in whole or in part in any form. · SIMON & SCHUSTER BOOKS FOR YOUNG READERS is a trademark of Simon & Schuster, Inc. For information about special discounts for bulk purchases, please contact Simon & Schuster Special Sales at 1-866-506-1949 or business@simonandschuster.com. · The Simon & Schuster Speakers Bureau can bring authors to your live event. For more information or to book an event, contact the Simon & Schuster Speakers Bureau at 1-866-248-3049 or visit our website at www.simonspeakers.com. · Book design by Lizzy Bromley and Tony DiTerlizzi · The text for this book was set in Letterpress Text. · The illustrations for this book were rendered in Ticonderoga pencil on bond paper. · Manufactured in the United States of America · 0820 FFG · First Edition · 2 4 6 8 10 9 7 5 3 1 · CIP data for this book is available from the Library of Congress. · ISBN 978-1-4169-8316-3 · ISBN 978-1-4424-8649-2 (eBook)

"HAPPINESS . . .
not in another place
but this place,
not for another hour
but this hour."

—WALT WHITMAN

I Haven't Forgotten

(I KNOW, I KNOW . . . IT HAS BEEN
*some time since I, Flit Shrewsbury—royal historian
for the king—have shared a story of young Kenny
Rabbit. Although I've gathered all the details for
this adventure, I am more a participant than a nar-
rator. So, without further ado, my trusted apprentice
shall describe the events as they happened.)*

*You may have heard tale of Kenny and his close-
knit family, who live in Roundbrook. It is a quaint,
circular-shaped town. Parrish Creek runs right
through the middle of it.*

I Haven't Forgotten

If you asked him, Kenny would say his best friend is Grahame, the kindhearted dragon, who arrived on Old Rabbit Farm several years ago and much to the distress of the local townsfolk. Thankfully, Kenny and his family and friends (as well as the retired knight Sir George) put on a Performance of a Lifetime to show that, in reality, not all dragons are the vicious beasts depicted in fairy tales.

After visiting with His Majesty, King Stonehorn, and the Royal Family, Kenny and company returned home to their sleepy little town. Well, it was a sleepy little town until word spread that a friendly fire-breathing dragon had taken up residence. Grahame's days were spent receiving far-flung fans and other adoring visitors, which suited him just fine. His friends transformed his cave into an amphitheater where Grahame would recite poetry and reenact scenes from his favorite plays.

The influx of tourists meant that Old Rabbit Farm could expand its enterprise. Not only did the sheep erect their own stables to spin wool, but several cows moved in. Now, a dairy farm requires extra paws to get chores done and, sure enough, with the addition of twelve *young bunnies to the Rabbit family, things are really hopping. (Get it? How I said "hopping"? You know, because they're rabbits and they . . . never mind.)*

Kenny certainly has had to adjust to his new home life, suddenly overrun with a dozen sisters. Simply remembering who's who is a chore unto itself: there's Karen, Kammie, Kettie, Katy, Kizzy, Kitty, Katherine, Kelly, Katrina, Kendall, Kirsten, and Kaye.

Our story begins with the entire Rabbit family climbing aboard their sheep-drawn cart to attend Roundbrook's annual Harvest Festival.

I. Wait for Me

"HURRY, MA!" THE FRONT DOOR banged shut behind Kenny's father, who scooped up an armload of bunnies on his way to the cart. "I don't want to be late like we were for the Corncob Festival."

"We've got plenty of time." Kenny's mother tightened the knot on her kerchief, then began helping each of her little ones onto the cart. "Careful now, Katy, don't step on your sister."

"I'm Kammie, Mama—she's Katy." The bunny pointed to another.

"Am not! She is." This bunny then pointed to

yet another, who had pried off the lid of a wooden crate on the back of the cart and began pulling out the woolen mittens and scarfs she'd found inside.

Their mother returned the clothes to the crate and secured the lid. "Don't muss the winter wear we knitted. We're donating those to the less fortunate, remember, Katy?"

"I'm Kendall, not Katy, and I don't wanna go to a festival!" The bunny folded her arms and scowled.

"Katy's with me, Ma," said Kenny Rabbit over the din. He hopped down from the porch with one little sister perched on his shoulders and a kit under each arm. Yet another rode on his foot, clutching his leg. He slogged over to the cart, where they scrambled off him and onto the others.

Kenny joined his parents at the front seat of the cart.

"Mama," said one of the bunnies. "How come he gets to sit up there with you?"

"I wanna sit up there too," said another, and climbed toward the front seat.

"You'll sit down right where you are, missy," their mother replied. "When you're older, you can ride up here. After all, Kenny is almost finished with school while you all have just begun preschool."

"Thank goodness," said Kenny's father under his breath. "I can finally get my work done in peace and quiet." He patted the sheep. "You good to go, Merino?"

"I think I can haaandle it," replied the sheep. He trotted down the drive, pulling the overloaded cart behind him.

The morning mist lifted to reveal leaves of orange, gold, and scarlet speckled across Shepard's Hill. The cart creaked past wilting wildflowers and weeds that drooped over the dirt road. Hidden under swaying blooms of goldenrod, a trio of crickets sang a slow, sad reminisce of summer days.

"Is Grahame joining us?" asked Kenny's mother.

"Yeah. He's going to meet me there."

"Good." She brushed fallen maple leaves from her dress. "He can help you keep an eye on your sisters while I judge the Annual Pie-Baking Contest."

Kenny groaned. "Aw, do I have to? We haven't hung out since school started and Charlotte's been—"

"No sass. You'll have plenty of time to goof around with your friends afterward."

"But can't Pa watch 'em?"

"I gotta bring the clothes over to the donations booth," said his father. "Jus' help me an' your mother out, 'kay, Kit? You won't have any other chores t'day."

"Okay. Okay." Kenny yielded, his paws up.

Merino's hooves clattered on the stone bridge that spanned Parrish Creek. Kenny peered over the edge to see Old Pops Possum fishing on the bank below. Kenny liked seeing Pops in the same spot he'd fished at for as long as he could remember. Old Pops tipped his hat as they went by and Kenny waved.

"Who is it?" Kendall watched Kenny. "I wanna say hi!" All twelve sisters leaned over the side of the cart and waved at Pops. "Helloooo!" they called down. Startled by this outburst, Pops dropped his fishing rod in the creek.

Kenny's father steered their cart through the crowded streets that led into Roundbrook. "Wow! Where'd all these folks come from?"

"I haven't seen it this busy since the parade for George," added his mother.

The town's welcome sign was decorated with bales of hay, piles of pumpkins, and stalks of dried corn. Behind it lay the commons, which were bordered with colorful tents and game booths. Carnival rides spun, wheeled, and whirred at the center of the field. Kenny's father thanked Merino and hitched the cart while Kenny hopped down to help his sisters out. He heard a deep inhalation of breath over his head.

"Don't you love the smell of fried food?" Grahame waved the scent toward his flaring nostrils.

"As far as I'm concerned, everything should be cooked in a fryer."

"Yeah it should!" Kenny rubbed his paws together. "Okay, I think we need to ride the Ferris wheel first, or maybe the Whip, or maybe we could go find Charlotte or—"

"Gam!" Kenny's sisters sprang from the cart and hopped around the towering teal dragon. They sang, "Gam's here! Gam's here! Gam's here!"

"It's not Gam, it's Grahame," said Kenny. "Like the cracker."

Grahame patted each bunny on the head. "They've been calling me Gam since they were wee cotton puffs. I rather like it." His prehensile tail delivered a tray overloaded with carnival treats. "Who wants funnel cake?" he asked.

"Me! Me! Me!" the sisters clamored, their paws outstretched.

Grahame handed out hunks of funnel cake to Kenny's sisters before stuffing his own face with pretzels, fried dough, and cotton candy. He spoke through a mouthful of food. "So, wud wide are we do-wing firth?" Powdered sugar puffed from his mouth like smoke.

"Don't eat too much junk food." Kenny's mother snatched the funnel cake from her daughters. "You'll get a stomachache."

"Maybe just a little heartburn," Grahame said with a burp. A flame danced on his tongue and Kenny snorted with laughter.

Kenny's mother shook her head at their sophomoric humor, then kissed her kits goodbye. "Do as your brother says. I'll see you soon."

Kenny's father picked up the stack of boxes from the cart. "Okay, Kit. I'm goin' to drop off Ma's donations, and then I'm gonna git some apple fritters. Don't let any of yer sisters run off." He called over his shoulder as he wobbled off, "Grahame, give 'im a hand. He's gonna need it."

"You're looking at Roundbrook's best bunny-sitter. Do not fret," Grahame said with a salute. Kenny smirked. While watching his parents disappear into the crowd, he listened to screams of delight mixed with calliope music as rides whipped and whorled their passengers.

One of Kenny's sisters, Kitty, tugged his paw and pointed to a passing festivalgoer adorned with a silly balloon hat. "I want one of those hats!"

"Okay, we'll get one later, after Grahame and I—"

"Look! You get 'em over there." Another sister, Katherine, pointed to a gaudy fellow surrounded by a horde of youngsters, twisting long, colorful balloons into shapes.

"Ugh," said Kenny. "But look at that crowd. We'll be waiting forever. Let's go on a ride instead."

"I wanna funny hat!" the sisters whined in unison.

"Well, Ma said you have to do what I say. *I say* we're going on a ride," replied Kenny.

"Balloon hats would be fun," said Grahame. "Besides, how can you say no to these sweet faces?"

"It's not hard," replied Kenny.

"Aw, come on." Grahame spoke in a persuasive tone. "You know you want one."

Kenny gave a reluctant smile to his friend and nodded. "Okay, let's go."

Grahame addressed the sisters. "All right, my little maidens, who wants to ride the dragon train?" The bunnies squealed with excitement and climbed onto Grahame's tail.

Kenny led them toward the balloon twister. Pulling a handful of coins from his pocket, he handed one to each of his sisters as they hopped off Grahame. "Drop this in his hat, then tell him what you want him to make for you. And hurry up, okay?"

Kenny and Grahame watched as the balloon twister created swords, flowers, and animals for all twelve sisters. While they were busy showing one another their creations, the twister presented Kenny and his friend with complimentary balloons.

"A pair of rabbit ears for Grahame the Great," he said, tying the ears to Grahame's horns. "And a dragon helmet for Kenny Rabbit."

Donning the ridiculous hat, Kenny cleared his throat and stood tall. "I am Gam, the benevolent dragon, and I just love toasting crème brûlée with my nose fire."

"And I am Kenny Rabbit, bibliophile, bicycle enthusiast, and big brother to twelve silly little sisters," said Grahame, imitating Kenny's voice.

"You guys are the ones who are silly!" said Kaye. The sisters laughed and chased after their brother, who ran round and round Grahame.

"Kenny Rabbit, are you having fun without me?"

Kenny turned to see Charlotte's smiling face. Her cotton dress fluttered in the breeze while she sipped a bottle of root beer from a striped paper straw. "You ran right past me and you weren't gonna say hi?" she said.

The tips of Kenny's ears grew hot under his balloon hat. He gave a sheepish smile and waved. "Hi, Char—"

"Kenny. I haffa go to the bathroom." His sister Katrina appeared from nowhere and tugged on his shirt.

"In a minute, okay? Look who's here! It's Char—"

"I haffa go now!" His sister started dancing in circles. Kettie and Kizzy joined her, announcing that they, too, had to go.

"It's all right, Kenny." Charlotte tried to conceal her giggle. "I'll wait."

Kenny blushed but said nothing. He took his sisters by the paw and rushed off to find the outhouses.

"Charlotte sure is nice," said Kettie. "I wanna be like her when I grow up."

"Me too," the others chimed in as they entered the outhouse.

"Just hurry up, okay?" Kenny closed the door behind them. While he waited for his sisters, he watched Charlotte from across the commons. She began chattering with a group of friends that he didn't recognize. They were probably her new classmates from her new school.

You see, Kenny had been looking forward to finally attending the same school as Charlotte, but before the school year started, her parents switched her to another with a more "robust arts program." Nowadays Kenny scarcely saw her. And when he did, all she talked about was her new school.

He watched Charlotte follow her friends to the roller coaster.

So much for waiting for me, he thought.

II. This Should Be Fun

"HEY! KINNY!" PORKY CALLED AS he jogged across the fairgrounds. The red ribbon pinned to his shirt matched the cherry pie filling smeared all over his face. Beside him, waving a spindly arm, was Polly, another classmate from school.

The outhouse door flung open and out hopped Kenny's sisters. "Polly's here!" they shouted.

"Hi!" Polly replied with a wide smile.

"Lookit!" A panting Porky pointed to his ribbon.

"I jist took second place in tha pie-eating contest."

"You should have seen it," said Polly in an excited tone. "I've never witnessed anyone ingest that many mixed-berry pies in sixty seconds."

"'Cept for my pa, who took first place," added Porky with pride. He noticed Kenny's balloon hat. "Whoa! You got yerself one fine hat. Where'd you git it?"

"The balloon man made it," said Katrina.

Kenny tried to get a word in. "He's over there. He—"

"Looky! He made me an ax." His sister swung it around, trying to chop her sibling.

"Hey, Porky! Hey, Polly!" Charlotte joined them, clutching coiled strips of colorful tickets.

"What happened to your new friends?" said Kenny.

"Abbie Alderose had to leave early and gave me her extra tickets. Do y'all want to ride the Ferris wheel?"

"Sure!" Porky tore off a pair of tickets and handed one to Polly.

"Thanks, Charlotte!" Polly gave her a quick hug.

Before Kenny could get a word in, Grahame marched up with Kenny's sisters bouncing behind him and each waving their balloon sculpture. "Arrah!" said Grahame. "Do I spy fair Charlotte? And here's the royal food taster, Porky, with his loyal friend Polly."

Everyone greeted Grahame with hugs and started talking to him all at once. Porky and Polly recounted the pie-eating contest while Charlotte described her drama club. *Of course she's talking about that*, Kenny thought. He was continually bopped and bonked by his balloon-wielding sisters as they marched around the dragon.

Kitty, the sassiest, stopped marching and began poking at Kenny repeatedly. "I wanna go on that ride," she said, pointing at the carousel.

Charlotte knelt down, showing off her wad of tickets. "How about we all go on the Ferris wheel?"

"I don't wanna go on a Ferris wheel," Kitty said. "I wanna go on that one!" Her finger firmly pointed at the carousel. "Me too!" the others chorused.

Kenny exchanged a glance with Charlotte. "Okay," he said, "how about we go on the carousel *after* the Ferris wheel?"

"I wanna go on the carousel NOW!"

Kenny's voice rose with frustration. "Well, we already did what you wanted, so now you have to do what I want. And I want to—"

"I got 'em." Grahame scooped up Kitty. "You go ahead."

"Are . . . are you sure?" said Kenny.

"What are friends for?" Grahame winked and led the bunnies toward the entry line. "Go on. Have fun."

"Come on, Kenny." Charlotte took him by the paw.

The friends piled into the ornate car of the Ferris wheel and peered over the edge as it rose up and over the crowds below. As soon as they were off the ground, Porky started rocking the car back and forth.

"You think I can make it flip? Or fall off?" he asked.

"No." Polly peered down. "This thing is constructed from an alloy steel. It's bolted and pinned. We're not going anywhere."

"How's the old school, Kenny?" asked Charlotte. "Any good teachers? You don't have Mr. Mallard this year, do you?"

Sometimes it was hard for Kenny to look directly at Charlotte and not lose his train of thought—especially when she was sitting right next to him. "Nope. Mallard retired and moved away. We have a new teacher, Mrs. Terrapin. She's a slow talker, but she seems nice."

"Lucky. It figures Mean Mr. Mallard would retire right after I leave." She rolled her eyes. "Omigosh! Did Grahame tell you? My new school has the most amazing theater and drama club. We've just started our production of *The Taming of the Shrew* and I'm going to make the costumes! Isn't that exciting?"

"Great. So, I guess you'll be spending even more time with your new friends?" Kenny propped his chin in the palm of his paw.

"Yes, you *have* to meet them! They are *so* talented. My one friend does incredible things with makeup. He painted me green, just like the Wicked Witch of the West, and then . . ."

Charlotte continued on about the play and the fabrics she planned to use for the costumes. Kenny had no idea what half the stuff was she was talking about. He wanted to ask, but she yakked nonstop for the duration of the ride, leaving him no opportunity.

As soon as the Ferris wheel came to a stop, Kenny couldn't hop off fast enough. He hurried through the crowd to Grahame, leaving Charlotte and the others trailing behind.

"Oh, thank goodness you're back." The dragon was surrounded by a ring of bawling bunnies. "There was a dispute among your sisters over who would ride the unicorn." He pointed to the carousel. "It seems no amount of cotton candy will sate their anger. Apologies, Kenny. I tried."

Kenny's mother walked out of the crowd, followed by his father. "It's okay, Grahame, I'll take it from here." She gathered her cranky bunnies. "It's time to go, my kits."

"Mama, no! I don't wanna go!" Kendall started thumping the ground with her foot in a tantrum. Several of her sisters joined in.

"We're going and that's final," Kenny's father said in a stern voice. "Son, you and Grahame be home by dinner, okay?"

"Okay," Kenny said as he watched his parents drag his twelve sisters toward the cart. He turned to Grahame. "Finally! It's just you and me."

Before Grahame could reply, the rest of their friends caught up with them, including Charlotte, who was still talking about her play. As far as Kenny could tell, she didn't think anything had gone wrong on the Ferris wheel. *Fine*, he thought. *Let's all just have some fun.*

They strolled past rows of carnival games adorned in flashing lights.

"Step right up, lad!" A scruffy barker juggled red rubber balls. "It's just three empty milk bottles. Knock 'em over and win a prize for the lucky lady!"

Another called from across the aisle, "Who's the boss at Ring Toss? You are! You are!"

"Hey," said Charlotte. "I still have just enough tickets for each of us to try a game."

The group scanned the midway, each in a different direction. Kenny's ears perked at a distinct twang coming from the striped tent up ahead. A large bull's-eye stood at the entrance. "Guys." He pointed. "Look!"

"An archery range!" Porky dashed past. "I'm so in. Let's go!"

"Now, *this* should be fun." Grahame walked with Kenny. "I've always wanted to try shooting a bow and arrow."

"I wonder. Are they using recurve bows or European straight bows?" asked Polly as she fell in line behind them.

"Ooo! We'll be like Robin Hood and his Merry Men," said Charlotte. She handed the last of her tickets to the outfitter, who was standing in front of the archery tent.

The outfitter sized each of them for a bow,

using a small stepladder to measure Grahame. He pulled out a large but slender bow, which was taller than Kenny. "I think this longbow would work best for you," he said, and handed it to the dragon.

Grahame pulled the bowstring back. In a dramatic voice he spoke. "Let us not footle about, Kenny, for we must forfend all evil, wherever it may lurk."

"Hold your horses, Little John." The outfitter chuckled and equipped the rest of the group with their bows and quivers. "Okay, you're all set. Go on down to the range and Link will show you what to do."

Kenny and his friends walked under a decorative banner that read BRAVE ARCHERS, YOU MUST PROTECT ROUNDBROOK! They exited the archery tent and entered the range. Festivalgoers of all ages shot arrows down a roped-off field. Towering stacks of hay stood at the far end with targets placed in front. Kenny could hear the repetitive thumping sound of arrows hitting their mark. His gaze followed an arrow whizzing through the air, piercing its target: a wooden cutout of a hydra,

viciously baring its fangs from its many heads. Next to it stood a spitting manticore and a stern-faced griffin, its talons outstretched. *Oh, please don't let there be a dragon, please don't let there be a dragon.* Kenny's eyes swept over the range.

"I got 'im!" A young lad pointed at his arrow lodged between a basilisk's yellow eyes.

"Nice shot." His father tousled his hair.

Porky twanged his bowstring. "Oh yeah! We're shootin' monsters."

"Porky!" Charlotte gave him a disapproving look.

"Maybe we shouldn't do this." Kenny turned to his friends, but it was too late. Grahame was standing right behind him, his eyes wide and his face pale.

"Oh hey, Kenny. Hey, Grahame!" The archery instructor, Link, approached the group with a

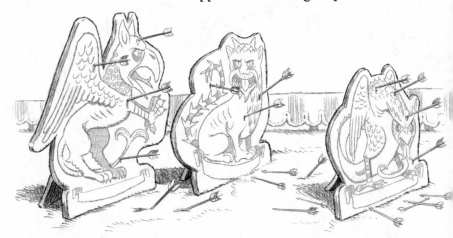

friendly smile. "You guys ready to get started?"

"Seriously?" Charlotte put her paws on her hips.

"Aw, don't be nervous," Link said. "You'd be surprised how many discover that they're a pretty good shot once they take aim."

"It's not *that*." Kenny pointed downrange. "It's what everyone is shooting at: the targets. You couldn't just use a bull's-eye?"

Link gave a puzzled expression. His gaze shifted to the targets, then back again to Kenny and Grahame. "Oho! I get it. We're just having some fun. There's no dragons."

"But what about the others?" said Kenny.

"Those monsters?" said Link. "They are nothing like you, Grahame. Nothing like you at all."

Grahame handed his bow and quiver to Link, his lemony eyes downcast. "You don't know that," he said.

Kenny handed his equipment over as well.

His friends followed suit.

III. *Anywhere but Here*

THE LOW AFTERNOON SUN CAST long shadows on the dirt road as Kenny and Grahame walked home. The cheery song of a chickadee did little to soothe their frustrations.

"Why couldn't the targets be lemon meringue pie, English trifle, or even schnecken? That would be much more fun to shoot arrows at," said Grahame, finishing a caramel apple.

"Especially if you were awarded the real McCoy when you hit a bull's-eye." Kenny picked up a pinecone.

"Now you're talking!"

They crossed the bridge over the creek. "I've known Link since I was a kit. I'm surprised at him. After all, he was at our performance years ago. He knows better." Kenny threw the pinecone into the water below.

"Well, then he's a bit daft, isn't he? A less tolerant drake would've bowstringed him right then and there, I tell you." Flames flickered in Grahame's nostrils. "Fortunately for him, I'm no villain."

Kenny patted Grahame reassuringly. "Link knows you, but I don't think the thought that there may be others like you even occurred to him."

"Yes. Perhaps." The flames died down in Grahame's nose. "You know, I used to be friends with hydras, hippogriffs, and all manner of magical folk. I was on good terms with a griffin named Leonardo, who was a bit full of himself . . . but that's beside the point."

"Trust me, I think Link got the message loud and clear when we all walked out." Kenny adjusted his balloon hat.

"Thanks," said Grahame. "Us vicious beasts need to stick together."

The morning after the festival, Kenny lugged a
bucket, oilcan, and toolbox across his backyard to
a dilapidated motorcar parked in the open carriage
house. He studied a crumpled sheet of paper laid
out on the car's rusted hood, tracing his finger over
a diagram of the engine for the Jolt Runabout
automobile.

Grahame rolled a pair of tires into the carriage
house and leaned them against the roofless car.
"Do you think we'll get this running today?"

"I'm sure gonna try." Kenny pushed up the
sleeves of his coveralls. "But it's a little tricky
without the owner's manual."

"There's not a used copy at the bookshop?"

Kenny unclipped the hood. It creaked in
protest as he flipped it open. "George will know.
I'll ask once he's back from his trip."

"By the by, when is he due to return from his
latest expedition?"

"Any day now." Kenny gripped the brass radiator cap on the front of the car. He tried to wrench
it loose, but it would not budge. "Who knows,"

he said, straining, "maybe he'll have located more dragons."

"That seems unlikely." Grahame let out a smoky sigh. He grasped the cap. It squeaked with each turn, but he easily unscrewed it. "He's been on so many expeditions and found no one. I fear I may be the last, a lone troubadour reciting the poetry and songs of all that once was."

Kenny's father wandered out from the barn with a bucket in hand. "I shoulda known you'd be out here fiddlin' with this Tin Lizzie. If you ask me, it's a waste of your hard-earned money."

"Polly's uncle gave me a good deal," Kenny replied. "If I can get it running, it'll be much faster than my bike."

"But not as reliable as ol' Merino," said his father as he lit his pipe. "Jus' last month I heard that one of these newfangled auto carriages blew up, right in the middle of town." He exhaled a puff of smoke. "It was hissing and whistling like a devil on fire. The car overheated and *BOOM*—a blast-plosion! A hunk of the engine shot right out of the hood like a cannonball. That dang hunk is still lodged in the brick wall of the Roundbrook Inn."

"Stuck in the wall?" Kenny chuckled. "I dunno about that, Pa."

"It's true!" Kenny's father pointed at him with the stem of his pipe. "You ask Pops Possum. He seen it with his own eyes."

"Oh, *Pops Possum*: Roundbrook's resident fabulist," Grahame announced in a dramatic tone. Kenny snickered.

Kenny's father waved off their teasing. "Go on, then. You two dunderheads keep wastin' yer time with that thang, but don't come cryin' to me when it explodes in yer face." He filled his bucket and walked back to the barn.

Kenny laughed to himself as he pulled a rag from his back pocket and wiped grime from the oily engine. Grahame unlatched the glove box and removed a pair of driving gloves, dusty goggles, and a road map. "Ooo!" He unfolded the map. "Where shall we go once we're—"

Grahame was interrupted by Kenny's sisters shouting at one another in the house, followed by the sound of a dish breaking. Soon Ma Rabbit could be heard scolding the lot of them.

"Some days I just wanna go anywhere but here," Kenny muttered. "Just you and me."

Grahame nodded, understanding. "I suppose it's a bit much with all these little kitlings invading your space."

"You have no idea." Kenny furiously scrubbed the engine.

"I wish I had a sibling."

"I know twelve sisters you can have."

Grahame smiled. "I actually enjoyed playing with them yesterday, despite their outbursts."

Kenny paused from cleaning. "Thanks for watching them at the festival. I needed a break."

"Think nothing of it. Besides, it allowed you to spend time with Charlotte. How is she faring at her new school? Did she tell you about the play?"

"Oh, she told me." Kenny rummaged through the toolbox. "That's all she talked about. That's all she ever talks about."

"She couldn't wait to tell you. I know you

don't see each other as much, but—"

"I don't want to discuss it." Kenny tucked the engine diagram back in his pocket. "Okay, I changed the oil, replaced the flat tires, and added fresh water to the radiator."

"Which will keep the engine cool, right?" said Grahame. "We don't want any blast-plosions."

Kenny giggled as he slid into the driver's seat. "There will be no blast-plosions today. But I did reconnect the wires for the horn." As he pressed a large button on the steering column, the horn cried, *A-HOO-ga! A-HOO-ga!*

"What a great sound," said Grahame, smiling.

"I love it," replied Kenny with a mischievous grin. He pressed the horn again and again. "D'ya think Pa likes it?"

Grahame started laughing out loud. "Oh, I am sure he just *loves* it."

"Kenny Rabbit!" His mother's voice cut through their laughter. "Stop honking that infernal horn. If you wake your sisters from their nap, *you* can deal with them."

"Sorry, Ma," said Kenny.

"Apologies, milady," added Grahame. They

stifled their sniggering as she shut the kitchen window and locked it.

"So . . . where were we?" asked Kenny.

"Is there gasoline in the tank?" asked Grahame.

"Yup." He reached in the backseat of the car and pulled out an old fruit crate. "Let's see . . . ," he said as he rooted around. "Kerosene for the lights, rope, motor oil . . . aha!" He pulled out the starting crank. "Should we see if it runs?"

Grahame clapped in anticipation. "Ooo yes!"

The two friends pushed the car out of the carriage house and parked it in the shade of a bright yellow sugar maple—a spot where they often relaxed together. Kenny inserted the crank into the front of the car.

"Remember," said Grahame. "Polly's uncle told you to use your left paw when starting it. And don't forget to tuck in your thumb."

"Got it." Kenny gripped the hard rubber handle. He jerked the crank in a clockwise motion. The engine puffed, then went silent.

He tried again.

And again.

And again.

Nothing.

Grahame knelt down to get a closer look.

"Maybe I missed something." Kenny rubbed his paw.

"It won't start?" his mother called from the back porch while his father watched. The sheep and cows poked their heads out of the barn.

"Let me give it a try." Grahame grasped the handle with his large fingers and turned it. The car coughed and sputtered but did not start.

Kenny jumped behind the steering wheel and

pushed up the gas throttle. "Okay. Try it again."

The car backfired with a *BANG*. Kenny's mother scurried back into the house. His father munched on a stalk of grass and continued watching.

"One more time," said Kenny.

Grahame nodded and cranked. The engine chugged to life.

"Yes! Yes! Yes!" Kenny revved the noisy engine for several minutes. It gasped, choked, and clunked out, releasing a thick cloud of black exhaust.

Grahame frowned as he waved it away. "Yuck. That smoke tastes different from dragon fire. Are you sure this thing is safe?"

Kenny replied, "I thought—"

A loud pop interrupted him as the radiator cap blew off, followed by a geyser of boiling water. "Ugh!" Kenny tugged his ears in frustration. "Why does it keep overheating?"

"Don't worry." Grahame patted him on the head. "We'll figure it out."

His mother opened the kitchen window and called out, "Kenny, can you come inside?"

He sighed loudly, slid out of his car, and plodded toward the house.

"You all right, Kit?" his father asked as he passed.

Kenny nodded glumly and went inside. His mother was chatting with a carrier pigeon at the front door.

". . . Thanks again, Ernest. He's right here. I know he'll be delighted to get the news." She turned to Kenny. "You're lucky your sisters slept through all that racket you were making."

"I'm sorry, Ma."

"You know, sometimes I need a break too."

"You're right," he replied. "I'll be more mindful."

"Good. This is for you." She handed a postcard to Kenny. "It's George. He's back."

-37-

IV. Some News

KENNY PUMPED THE PEDALS ON
his bike as he rode down the well-traveled streets
of Roundbrook. The quiet Sunday afternoon gave
the appearance of a town abandoned, save for the
occasional shopper. A train whistle shrilled in the
distance as a train clanked along the tracks.

The paperboy waved from the newsstand.
"Hey, Kenny! I hear George is back."

"Yup. He got in yesterday." Kenny coasted by.
"I'm on my way to see him now."

"I can't wait to hear all about his trip. See ya
later!"

Some News

Kenny parked his bike against the lamppost outside the Burrow Bookshop. Hopping up the steps, two at a time, he passed a faded sign that hung on the storefront window:

CLOSED

Traveling on Royal Business.
Will reopen once I return.
Thank you for your patronage.
—Sir George E. Badger
P.S. If it's a book emergency,
contact Kenny Rabbit, Esq.

The familiar tinkling sound of the bell announced Kenny's arrival as he entered the shop. The scent of used books and aged wood greeted him. He flipped the sign to OPEN before skipping down aisles of shelves to the back of the store. George was opening boxes full of new books in the cramped stockroom.

"My squire!" George's gravelly voice was soft but spirited. He clasped Kenny's shoulders and studied him. "Come in, come in." The badger's

aging eyes still sparkled behind the smudged lenses of his glasses and his clothing sagged, suggesting that the muscled brawniness of his youth had begun to leave him. George went on, after a moment. "Thank you for taking care of the shop in my absence, even if it was sporadic. I truly appreciate it."

"I tried to come by when I could," replied Kenny. "And Charlotte helped sometimes, but . . . she's been busy."

"So I hear. She stopped by earlier with her friends looking for a book on Shakespearean costume."

Kenny ignored this statement and continued. "Well, I'm glad you're back. It's not the same without you here."

"It is good to be back," George said with a faint smile.

Kenny detected a hint of sadness in George's voice but chalked it up to exhaustion from his travels. "So . . . *The King's Royal Bestiary*," he said. "I'm dying to know: What did you discover?"

George poured two cups of tea. He added a drop of honey before handing one to Kenny. "Well, for the past several years I have worked closely with the royal historian, Flit, on his research of mythical beasts. I traveled extensively throughout the kingdom in search of those, like Grahame, that were listed in the bestiary."

"I can't wait to update the text," said Kenny before sipping his tea.

"Flit has discovered that there was another bestiary, titled *The Book of Beasts*, written over three hundred years ago by an author named Nesbit."

"I've never heard of that one," said Kenny.

"Nor have I," replied George. "However, it appears that entire passages were copied from *The Book of Beasts* for *The King's Royal Bestiary*. This was common practice among authors back then, and it may explain the erroneous facts."

Kenny was too excited to drink his tea. "Wow. So, where did you find the original bestiary?"

George's bushy eyebrows furrowed. "Sadly, neither Flit nor I could locate a copy of *The Book of Beasts* . . . or any of the creatures it described. Our friend Grahame may very well be the last of his kind."

Some News

Kenny set down his tea. *The last of his kind.* Just like Grahame had said to him that morning. "Are you sure? You've searched everywhere?"

George nodded. "In every location that had a recorded sighting. But, mind you, all these sightings occurred ages ago."

"What about the author? Nesbit?" asked Kenny.

"Not much is known. Flit called upon the royal messengers to deliver a summons to all corners of the kingdom, hoping that perhaps one of Nesbit's living descendants may come forth and shed light on the whereabouts of the book. It's a long shot, but someone may have information; otherwise, it would appear that the expedition to update *The King's Royal Bestiary* is a failure."

They were quiet for a moment while Kenny absorbed all of this. The old knight clapped him on the shoulder. "Don't be so downhearted, lad," said George. "Grahame may not have others like him in his life, but he has you. That means a lot."

"Yeah . . . I guess you're right," said Kenny.

"Of course! By the way, where is the old fireball?" asked George.

"He said he'd stop by after his nap. He wanted

to be refreshed for tonight's visit." Kenny sipped his tea. "We've been busy all morning trying to get my car running."

"Ah yes, Charlotte told me about your latest project. Well, I can tell you that these horseless carriages are certainly all the rage. You should see the fancy one used to chauffeur the king. Did you get yours running?"

"For about a minute." Kenny frowned. "Without the owner's manual it has been tricky."

"Hmmm." George stirred his tea. "Did you go through the box of used manuals that we have here?"

"I wondered if we had any."

"We do. They're here . . . somewhere." George surveyed the heaps of books stacked on every surface. "I'll take a look around and see if I can't find them."

The front doorbell jangled as a mother and her pups entered the shop. George set down his teacup and shuffled over to greet his customers.

While he waited, Kenny grabbed a box from the stockroom and heaved it onto the counter. Inside were new copies of the latest bestseller—a novel about dinosaurs living in a Lost World.

Some News

Grahame might enjoy this one, he thought to himself. Leafing through the pages, he paused on an illustration depicting a mob of dragon-like pterosaurs attacking hapless adventurers. Kenny closed the book and stacked it with the rest on a display marked NEWEST ARRIVALS. At the far end of the store, behind the shelves of children's books, he could overhear the conversation.

"I want this one," a young voice said.

His mother replied, "I'm sorry, but we don't have enough money for that book. You'll have to choose one from the sale bin."

"But this is the one I want!"

George spoke up. "Hello there."

"Well, hello, George," said the mother. "Welcome back."

"Thank you," replied the old knight. "To celebrate my return, we are having a special sale. That's right, it's Family Book Day. I get to give one book to each family that visits my shop. And so, I shall give this one to you."

"Really?" the pup squealed.

"What do you say?" his mother asked.

"Thank you, Mister George."

The family filed out the front door, each holding on to one another's tail. At the front of the procession, the young pup was hugging a book so close to his chest that Kenny couldn't see the cover. The mother turned to George. "You really are a saint," she said, and pecked him on the cheek before leaving the shop.

The old knight closed the door behind them. He watched them leave through the front window. With a deep sigh he said, "I love this little town. I sure am going to miss it."

"Miss it?" said Kenny. "But you just got back."

"I know." George turned to him. His voice softened. "Kenny, I have some news."

"Wha . . . what is it?"

"The king has appointed me to his council. I shall serve as his royal advisor."

"That sounds great!"

"That it is." George knelt down and placed a paw on Kenny's shoulder. "But it means I'll be relocating back to the castle."

It was as if George had hurled a stone right into Kenny's stomach. "You're . . . moving?" was all he could squeak out.

George continued speaking, but Kenny heard only fragments. The old knight gestured to the overloaded bookshelves surrounding him. "Honestly, lad, this is too much for a fellow of my age to keep up with."

Kenny avoided George's gaze and looked down at the slats on the floor.

"I know this is a lot for you. I am truly sorry to leave, but when the king calls, I must answer. Do you understand?"

Kenny sniffled and nodded. "Yes. I understand." But he didn't. Not really. He knew it was the grown-up thing to say and it was what George wanted to hear, so he said it.

"There's a good lad." George went to hug him.

Kenny hardly returned the gesture. "I have to go."

V. The Other Half of Hello

KENNY BARELY ATE THE RATATOUILLE served for dinner that night. His sisters' antics kept both his parents so occupied that there was no time to talk about George leaving. While his mother put his sisters to bed, Kenny cleared the table and stacked the dirty dishes on the counter. His father was standing at the sink, scrubbing a charred baking dish.

"Not yer day today, is it, Kit?"

Kenny said nothing. The news of George leaving, mixed with Charlotte spending time with her new friends, stewed in his brain. He furiously wiped off his sisters' mess from the table with a damp dishrag.

His father let out a long sigh. "I know I gave you a hard time this mornin'. It's just that I don' like these blasted automobiles. I see more 'n' more of 'em driving willy-nilly on the road ev'ry day, disturbing the peace an' quiet." He rinsed the dishes. "But I know one thing: they're here to stay and there ain't nothin' I can do about it. That's the thing about change, son. It happens whether you like it or not. You can spend yer time fightin' it, or you can jus' accept it."

"I don't want to accept that George is moving away," said Kenny. It felt good to disagree with his father even though Kenny knew he had nothing to do with why he felt the way he did.

"I know it can seem overwhelmin' in times like this. You do yer best and remain true to who you are. Sometimes a bit of good comes with change."

Kenny threw down the dirty dishrag. "What good comes from my friends leaving me?"

"What about ol' Grahame? He's yer best friend and he's still here. I don't think he'll ever leave . . . at least not while Ma keeps cooking for 'im."

Kenny gave a slight smile.

His father dried his paws and turned to him. "It's never easy to say goodbye, Kit. But it is the other half of hello. Once we say hello, the other half eventually follows."

Kenny nodded in understanding.

His father resumed washing. "You'll see ol' George again, and Charlotte, too. Like you, she's busy with school."

"I know. It's just . . . hard sometimes."

"It is. But d'ya know what's easy? Sayin' hello again after you've had to say goodbye." His father placed the dishes on the drying rack. "The king himself has asked George to come advise him. That's a tremendous honor. You should be happy for yer friend . . . not sulkin' around like a soggy raincloud."

***

His chores now finished, Kenny walked out to the carriage house, where his dead car was parked. The scent of the overheated engine still hung in the air. He climbed in the driver's seat and closed his eyes.

In his mind, the engine was purring as he steered his shiny polished car down the drive. Grahame held the open road map in the seat next to him. George, Charlotte, and the rest of Kenny's friends and family were tearfully bidding them farewell. "Bye!" he called to them. "We have to leave." They pleaded for him to stay, but he and Grahame continued until they drove out of sight.

The following week, Kenny was so busy with schoolwork, chores, and watching his sisters that he hardly saw Grahame, let alone had any spare time to tinker with his car. He tried not to think about George moving away, even when his parents brought it up. However, by the weekend it was unavoidable: Kenny's mother had invited the old knight over to dinner.

The entire family sat around the table, with George at the head. Grahame took his usual spot outside the Rabbit house, his large face protruding through the open dining room window. "This butternut squash soup is simply divine." He licked the spoon held in his coiled tail.

"Why, thank you, Grahame." Kenny's mother had hardly sat down the entire meal and was wiping food from each of her daughters' faces with the corner of her apron. "It was my grandfather's old recipe. His secret was to add an apple."

"I thought I tasted a hint of Granny Smith in there," said Grahame with a wink. Everyone laughed, including Kenny.

"It is a fine meal, indeed," George added. He pushed back his chair and stood, holding his mug high. "Rabbit family, I thank you for this kingly feast and for your warm hospitality over these many years. I shall miss our engaging conversations, and Ma's splendid cooking, until my next visit."

Everyone clinked their glasses and drank.

"My dear Grahame." George handed him a gift-wrapped book. "I thank you for your open mind and open heart. You've certainly taught this old knight not to judge a book by its cover."

"Hear, hear!" Grahame said. Everyone clinked their glasses and drank.

George turned to Kenny. "To my fellow book lover, chess partner, and squire: I thank you for your bravery, candor, and most importantly, your friendship. Yours is a treasure that can never be replaced."

Kenny smiled back at the old knight even though it was difficult.

"I have for you, this." George pulled an envelope from his vest pocket and presented it to him. "May it remind you that, though many stories have been told, yours is far from over."

Kenny felt all eyes upon him as he accepted the envelope.

"What's innit, Mama?" one of his sisters asked. She was answered with a shush.

George gestured to the envelope. "Go ahead, lad. Open it."

Kenny tore open the envelope. A large brass key with the letters *B.B.* worked into its decorative fob fell into his palm. He looked up at George, mouth agape.

"Yes," George said with a nod. "The shop is yours."

Kenny's mother gasped.

"I . . . I don't . . . think I can." Kenny stared at the key.

"Oh, it's not that hard," said George. "You're practically running it anyway."

Kenny placed the key on the table. "No. I don't think I can take this." He slid the key to George. "Not because I don't appreciate it, but . . . because I don't want you to go." He rushed up to the old knight and hugged him tight.

"You are a good lad, Kenny." George patted his back. "This town needs books and you're the one for the job. Charlotte said she'd be thrilled to work with you. Think about it, okay?"

Kenny wiped his eyes. "Okay."

George gave a crafty smile. "You know, we can talk about this further on our trip to the castle."

"*Our* trip?"

"Yes!" George clapped his paws together. "Right after you left the shop, I found a used copy of the owner's manual for your Jolt Runabout. I gave it to Grahame that evening. He burned the midnight oil to repair your automobile."

Kenny looked over at Grahame, who could not conceal his growing smile. "You fixed my car?"

"Surprise!" said Grahame. "Although, I just did the labor—you figured out what was wrong."

"I did?"

"Yup. Turns out it was a faulty water pump." Grahame spoke with the confidence of a seasoned auto mechanic. "I may have fixed some other stuff as well."

George extended a paw to Kenny. "Your parents are okay with you driving me up to the castle—"

"...as long as I tag along," continued Grahame.

"So . . . what do you say?"

Kenny looked to his mother and father. Both gave a nod of approval.

He beamed from ear to ear. "I say, when do we leave?"

VI. Royal Guests

THE THREE FRIENDS TRAVELED
the entire day to reach the castle by sunset, stopping only to refill the gasoline tank in the car.

Even through the dusty windshield, the
view of the castle against a backdrop of golden
rolling hills was spectacular. Limestone towers
and shingled spires stood high over the treetops.
Kenny's car chugged past a wrought-iron gate
and down a cobblestone drive toward the entrance.

"How I love this time of year," said Grahame
as he glided overhead. "The changing hues of the
fall foliage are always a sight to behold."

George recited from the passenger seat, "'Every leaf speaks bliss to me, fluttering from the autumn tree.'"

"Ah, there is such beauty in Brontë's words," replied Grahame. "Here's one for you: 'Wild is the music of autumnal wind among the faded woods.'" He flapped his great wings, causing the fallen leaves in the drive to lift and whorl in a rustled chorus.

George applauded. "William Wordsworth! One of my favorites. Well done!"

Kenny parked the car in a roundabout at the front of the castle. A tiered fountain sat at the middle of the circular drive with a bronze sculpture at its center. The ivy-covered façade was a deep green, as were the topiaries that frolicked in the surrounding gardens.

(By the way, Master Flit wanted me to tell you that here is where he enters the story.)

Flit stood on the stone steps of the entrance, waving to the trio. "There they are! Our royal guests: Master Kenny, the legendary Grahame, and Sir George E. Badger. Welcome to Castle Stonehorn!"

"Hello, sir!" George greeted Flit with a hearty handshake while Grahame swooped overhead and landed on the lawn.

Kenny hopped out of the car and stretched the driver's cramp from his leg. Despite the fact that he was here to say goodbye to George, he was excited to visit the castle once again. "Hi, Mr. Shrewsbury!" he said.

Flit shook his hand. "What a loyal bunch you are. I am thrilled that you've all decided to escort His Majesty's royal historian here, to his new residence."

George looked at Flit, confused. "Hold on, aren't *you* the royal historian?"

"Oh yes! Of course! And *you* are the royal advisor. Silly me." Flit ushered them up the steps. "We have a grand meal set in a unique place, which I've organized just for you."

"Ooo! What's for dinner?" Grahame rubbed his hands. "All that flying has made me hungry."

"Well, it is all of your favorites, of course," Flit replied with a wink. "The staff will see to your belongings, Sir George." He gestured to the car, and several footmen began to unpack it. "Don't worry about a thing. We'll have you settled in no time. Now, if you'll follow me, I'll show you to your lodgings, where you can freshen up before we dine."

<hr>

Flit collected the guests at suppertime and led them through the castle grounds. They passed down a hall flanked with polished suits of armor and intricate tapestries depicting mythical beasts.

Grahame stopped at one of the tapestries and squinted at the embroidered scene of a unicorn fenced in a garden. "I think I knew her. Sophia was her name. Lovely lass. We used to talk about gardening tips. I wonder what became of her."

"This way," Flit said, pushing open a pair of arched double doors. The words STONEHORN LIBRARY were carved in the lintel above.

The high, barrel vault ceilings of the library were decorated in brightly colored frescoes. Kenny became dizzy staring up at them as he followed Flit into the grand room. Rows of shelving cases lined the walls, towering up to the cornice, each stacked with books and ancient artifacts.

"Wow." Kenny ran his paw over the gilded lettering printed on the spines of encyclopedias.

"The royal treasury!" Grahame wriggled through the double doors into the room.

"There are over forty thousand titles here," said Flit with pride. "Many in multiple languages."

George let out a whistle. "That is a lot of books."

A resonant voice echoed throughout the room, "Do you feel at home yet, Sir George?" King Stonehorn entered with arms outstretched. He was accompanied by the queen and their two sons and young daughter. "You know, it was Queen Stonehorn who suggested I hire you."

"Well, she is the smart one." George kissed her paw.

The king laughed and clapped George on the shoulder. "It's good to have you back home, old boy."

As he watched the two friends embrace, Kenny tried not to look as sad as he felt. George was truly back home.

The king turned to Kenny and Grahame. "Welcome, lads. What do you think of our little soirée?" He gestured to a large dining table at

the center of the library. A lanky butler stood
at the foot of the table, supervising a flurry of
servants who were filling glasses and placing
silverware on folded cloth napkins. Stonehorn
continued, "It was all Flit's idea, of course. He
practically lives in here."

"Thank you for having us, Your Majesty,"
said Kenny. "And Your Highness," he added with
a bow. The royal family nodded and smiled.

"Yes, indeed!" said Grahame. "I can hardly
wait to—"

A loud rustle was heard above. All turned to

see what appeared to be a giant bat flap through the open doors of the library.

"Who is this?" asked the king.

The bat circled overhead, sending the servants scurrying. It was then that Kenny realized it was not a large bat at all, but some sort of enchanted flying book. A cloaked rider, perched on the book's spine, seemed small compared to the enormous flapping pages. The book snapped shut before landing on the marble floor, and the rider dismounted, securing the metal clasps of the leather-bound cover.

"Who dares to interrupt a royal proceeding?" said the queen. "And on a flying book! What sort of sorcery is this?"

Royal Guests

"Everyone, back!" George seized a sword from a display and stood at the ready between the strange rider and the royal family.

The rider spoke in a creaky tone and ambled toward the guests with the aid of a cane. "Oh, calm down. I'm not going to hurt anyone."

"I make the commands here and I say halt and reveal yourself, immediately!" The king pointed at the rider with his scepter.

"Of course, of course. I've forgotten how much to-do it is when dealing with the likes of you." Gnarled claws pulled off a wide-brimmed hat, revealing an elderly white-haired possum. She rummaged through her tattered cloak and produced a paper from a hidden pocket. The royal insignia could be seen on the broken wax seal. "I received your summons, Your Majesty."

"Summons?" said the king.

"Yes." The possum stared up at him. A cataract clouded one of her eyes. "Eldritch Nesbit, at your service."

VII. A Monster's Instincts

"*T*HE E. NESBIT?" FLIT HELD THE notice he'd sent out months ago. "Author of *The Book of Beasts?*"

She nodded.

"But . . . but it's been centuries since your book was printed."

Kenny's mind was reeling from the magic flying book and the ancient possum now standing before him. "How are you still . . . um, you know—"

"Alive?" She finished his sentence with a

toothy smile. "I have my secrets."

The king continued, "But how is it that you're here at this very moment?"

"Well, magic books only travel so fast," Nesbit replied with a chuckle. "I have been abroad for some time now, but your summons did find its way to me . . . and so, here I am."

"Your timing is fortuitous," added the queen.

"Oh, that's because you have a monster present." Nesbit pointed at Grahame with her cane. "I can smell them from miles away."

"Monster?" Grahame ruffled. "I prefer *arcane spirit*."

"Pfft!" Nesbit gave a dismissive wave.

"Now, now." The king gestured for all to calm down. "Grahame is no threat to us."

"Grahame, is it?" Nesbit took a seat at the dinner table. "With all due respect, Your Majesty, when was the last time *you* met a dragon?"

"When was the last time any of us did?" said George. "Besides Grahame, there are no more mythical beasts—no griffins, unicorns, basilisks. I've searched far and wide for any sign of them and turned up nothing."

"And you won't find them ever again." She lifted a silver cloche and plucked a braised carrot from the platter.

"Is that so?" said the king. He motioned for George to lower his sword.

"Yes. They've been gone now for decades, leaving our land for a safer one." Nesbit tasted the carrot. "That's better for you and it's better for them. Trust me, I know everything there is to know about monsters. *Everything.*"

"So . . . they're not extinct?" The way George said it made it seem as if he were unconvinced.

"No, no, they're not extinct." With the carrot in hand, she pointed to George and the sword still in his grip. "After all, I would never *kill* a monster . . . unlike some."

"Now, hold on—"

"Oh, do relax, loyal knight. You were likely following your orders. After all, most monsters were . . . unpredictable"—Nesbit bit the carrot in half—"and therefore dangerous to the populace."

"Well, the same could be said about the populace itself," said Grahame.

Nesbit nodded in agreement. "Too true."

"But that was so long ago," said the king.

Kenny added. "Things are different now."

"Are they?" asked Nesbit.

"They are, thanks to folks like young Kenny here," replied George.

Nesbit turned to Grahame. "*Draco antiquissimus*. Sometimes called the European wyrm. Sometimes the Olde-World wyrm. A mature male: you can tell by the iridescent scales."

Flit whispered behind his paw to the king. "Sire, she certainly knows a lot."

"Yes. I do. And I can tell you, things may be 'different' now, but they really haven't changed." Nesbit ran her fingers along Grahame's tail, her claws clicking on his scales. "You take this fine specimen, here."

"Oh, why, thank you." Grahame twinkled at the compliment.

"Not only does a dragon, like this one, crave beautiful things, but he needs to eat every few hours. It would be best to keep him away from your pretty little daughter, Your Majesty," she said with a purr. "He might get hungry for a midnight snack."

"What!? Don't eat me!" the king's daughter cried, and fled the room.

Grahame tried to stop her. "I wouldn't dare! Your Highness!"

Queen Stonehorn gave a dirty look to Nesbit and hurried after her daughter. Nesbit cackled at the chaos.

"Enough!" King Stonehorn bellowed. His eyes flashed in the candlelight.

Flit hesitated before approaching the king. "I . . . I believe it is a joke, sire," he said with a nervous laugh. "She certainly has quite a sense of humor for one so . . . so . . ."

"Out of touch," said Kenny.

Nesbit curtsied to the king. "I beg your pardon, Your Majesty. Apologies if I have offended your progeny by stating these simple facts."

"Here's a simple fact for you: watch your tongue or you shall lose it," said the king.

Nesbit regarded him for a moment, then composed herself. "All right, then. Let us get down to business: I have received your summons. What do you require of me?"

The king motioned to Flit, who stepped forward and cleared his throat. "His Majesty requests a copy of *The Book of Beasts* so that we may reprint it."

She shook her head. "Alas, I do not have a copy."

"Do you know where we could obtain one? Our library seems to be—"

"I haven't the slightest. Sorry." She turned to go.

"What about your flying book, there?" Kenny pointed to the large tome.

"The ancient information contained in there is forbidden. It is not for the likes of you," said Nesbit. She addressed the king. "Is that all?"

"Not exactly," said Flit. He pulled a familiar

book from a shelf and placed it on a nearby table. The title printed on the cover read *The King's Royal Bestiary*. "What we'd like to do, then, is have you update and edit this text."

Nesbit donned a pair of reading glasses and sat down. She clucked as she paged through the book. "My research, carelessly copied over and over like a lousy game of grapevine." She sniffed in disgust and closed the covers. "But it doesn't matter anymore. The monsters are long gone, much to everyone's delight. Why bother revising the text?"

"Well, for starters, not every 'monster' is gone," said Grahame. "After all, I'm still here."

". . . and the facts are inaccurate," added George.

"We want everyone to know the truth," said Kenny.

Nesbit removed her glasses and shook her head. "Facts to you are fiction to others. We see only what we want to see." She pointed to each of them in turn. "Are you a friend? Foe? Ruler? Subject? A monster or savior? It is all in the eyes of the beholder."

"But there is the truth," the king added. "And that is very important."

"So you say," replied Nesbit with a shrug.

"Watch it." George waved his sword. "You're speaking to royalty."

"There, there, Sir George," said the king. "I think we need to come to an understanding: let us work together to find a peaceful solution." He set down his scepter and poured wine for his guests. Handing a glass to Nesbit, he continued, "When I was young, I saw a rabbit—just like young Kenny here—with a single horn growing from its head."

"A unicorn-rabbit?" asked Kenny.

"An Al-mi'raj," said Nesbit.

King Stonehorn went on. "When I described what I'd seen to my friends, they laughed and teased me. When I told my parents, they praised my vivid imagination. And yet I knew what I'd seen. It was as real as you sitting here before me. Although, I confess, over the years I began to doubt my own memory and the existence of such creatures . . . that is, until Grahame came along.

"I felt a sense of wonder I'd not known for so long. There was still magic in the world, yet to be discovered. I saw how the very thought of that inspired my own calves. They wanted to know all about the horned rabbit . . . er, Al-mi'raj, that I'd seen all those years ago. And they believed every word of my story."

"So give them this." Nesbit gestured at *The King's Royal Bestiary*.

Kenny opened the bestiary and skimmed the text. When he reached the entry titled "Dragons," he read aloud, "All drakes kill."

"A flagrant untruth if ever there was one," said Grahame with certainty.

"A monster's instincts cannot be denied," said Nesbit.

"He's no killer." George pointed at Grahame, who was refolding the cloth napkins.

"Well, unless it's a soufflé, then . . . watch out!" Grahame bared his teeth and struck a dramatic attack pose.

"See what I mean? Food-motivated," said Nesbit with a satisfied smile.

"What? Wait, no," Grahame started.

King Stonehorn took a deep, calming breath before he spoke. "Lady Nesbit, since you are the only one with intimate knowledge of all mythical creatures and since you no longer have a copy of the tome my historian requires, I am asking you to update the information in *The King's Royal Bestiary*."

"Here's some information for you: all monsters are bloodthirsty," said Nesbit. "The sooner you accept that, the—"

The king slammed his paw on the table. "I don't want your opinion and I don't want your judgments. I just want the facts. That is my wish. Can you do this or not?"

Nesbit glanced at Grahame, then back at the king, her whiskers twitching in thought. "Very well." She shuffled back to her enormous book. Its cover thumped as she unfastened the clasps. "Give me a fortnight. It should provide me ample time to revise the manuscript."

"Good!" The king exhaled in relief. He clapped his paws. "It is settled, then. Flit, ready the printing presses for—"

"But you may not like these *facts* as they are described." Nesbit stepped onto her flying book. "The truth may only deliver unease to your subjects."

"Let me be the judge of that."

"As you wish," Nesbit said with a bow. "I will ask to stay the night if possible. I'd like to gather more research before I depart."

"Of course," replied the king.

"Thank you, Your Majesty," said Nesbit in a simpering manner. "With permission, I'll take your leave. Traveling has left this old possum so very weary."

"Yes, yes. Flit will arrange sleeping quarters for you."

The royal historian quickly exited the library. "I shall let the royal press know that the revised edition of *The King's Royal Bestiary* is underway!"

"I bid you all good evening," Nesbit said as her book flapped its great covers and flew from the room.

George returned the sword to its display stand. Kenny frowned as he watched Nesbit go.

"Monster, indeed! That witch has got some nerve." Grahame downed his drink.

"Do not fret, Grahame. Flit will oversee Nesbit's work. Any falsifications describing your folk will be rectified." King Stonehorn took his seat at the head of the table. "Now then, let us eat. Who is hungry?"

VIII. A Strange Murmur

THE ROYAL BALLROOM WAS THE perfect quarters for a dragon-size guest. As well, it was ornate, warm, and—most importantly— close to the kitchen. Kenny and George sat with Grahame at the hearth of a crackling fire and spoke in hushed tones.

"So . . . is she a sorceress or a witch?" asked Kenny.

"Hard to tell, lad. But I haven't seen the likes of her in a long, long time." George cradled his steaming mug of tea. "I still don't know how she's remained in the land of the living. If she indeed wrote *The Book of Beasts*, she'd be nearly three hundred years old."

"Flying books? Alive for centuries? She may be a witch, but that's not your run-of-the-mill witchcraft," said Grahame, shaking his head. "She's using powerful magic."

"Dark magic?" asked George.

"She's wearing black on brown. What do you think?" Grahame sipped his chamomile tea from a pewter pitcher. "Though, honestly, she should just pick a color story and stick with it."

Kenny spoke. "When we play cards, Mom's whiskers twitch—just like Nesbit's—when she bluffs. She was hiding something."

"Mages, whether benevolent or maligned, have many secrets," said Grahame.

George drained the last of his tea, then went on. "This could be bad news. It'd be best to keep an eye on her. Find out what she's up to."

"I think we steer clear of her and let Stonehorn deal with it," said Grahame.

Relaxing in the quiet room with his friends, Kenny felt a sense of comfort that he hadn't experienced in quite some time. He let out a yawn, lay back on his sleeping mat, and closed his eyes while listening to their voices. He pushed away the thought that George would not be coming back home with him. A low gurgle interrupted the conversation. Kenny opened one eye.

Grahame patted his stomach. "Time for a little more dessert." He winked at Kenny before slithering off to the kitchen.

George chuckled as he watched him go. "Well, I guess that old crone was right about one thing." He turned to Kenny. "Good night, young squire. Thanks for the escort. I'm glad it was you who brought me here."

"You're welcome," said Kenny, and pulled the blanket over his head.

Grahame's snoring was so loud that he didn't hear the twelve chimes that echoed throughout the ballroom, but it woke Kenny with a start. He rubbed the sleep from his eyes and, for a moment, forgot where he was. His friend was curled up around him like a gigantic cat. Kenny fluffed his pillow, trying to get comfortable, but he could not stop thinking about Nesbit.

A strange murmur echoed through the open doors. Kenny lit a candle and wandered down the stone corridor toward the library. His ears swiveled as he followed the sound, which led to a closed door, a beam of light glimmering from its keyhole. Tiptoeing to it, he peered inside.

Nesbit was in her quarters, seated with her back to the door. The room was lit by an eerie glow emanating from the giant book, which lay open in front of her. Kenny watched her silhouette dip a feather quill into an inkwell, then inscribe unrecognizable glyphs and mysterious diagrams onto the pages. She was chanting in a soft voice and in a tongue that he did not understand.

"*Mox draco flammas exspirans in meum librum inibit. . . .*"

In a spidery handwriting she wrote, *Grahame*.

Kenny gasped. Nesbit stopped and turned suddenly. Kenny jerked away from the keyhole. Holding his breath, he waited until the chanting began again and peeked into the room once more. Nesbit had resumed her writing, seemingly

oblivious to him. A large mirror, hanging on the opposite wall from the door, caught Kenny's eye. The reflection of the cover was backward, which made the title hard to read. Kenny squinted as Nesbit flipped through the book to reveal the title page:

The Book of Beasts by Eldritch Nesbit.

"Whatcha doing?" Grahame whispered from over Kenny's shoulder, causing him to jump with fright. He turned to see the dragon stuffing his face with a fancy fruit tart.

"Who's there?" Nesbit called from her room. The door cracked open and her bewhiskered face poked out. She peered down the dark corridor, but nothing could be seen except for the flickering shadows of the sconces.

As they scurried back to their quarters, Kenny and Grahame agreed to notify the king of their discovery first thing in the morning. They returned to the ballroom and closed the doors. Grahame, of course, was asleep in minutes while Kenny tossed and turned. His fitful slumber was interrupted by a dream: He was at school but could not seem to find an exit. One by one his friends left him, despite his pleas. The last to go was Grahame, leaving Kenny all alone.

He awoke at dawn to find that Grahame was not there. *Of course, he's at breakfast already*, he thought as he stretched. A footman entered the ballroom and stoked the fire.

"Good morrow, Master Kenny. We hope you had a restful sleep. Breakfast will be served at the top of the hour."

Kenny yawned. "I suppose Grahame is already there, waiting."

"Grahame, sir?" The footman paused in his chores. "I've not seen him yet this morning."

The hairs on Kenny's neck stood on end and his pulse quickened. He bolted across the ballroom and flung open the doors, nearly knocking over George and Flit standing at the entrance.

"My young squire!" George saw the anxious look on Kenny's face. "What's going on?"

Kenny pointed down the hall and spoke fast. "Last night . . . I think . . . Nesbit has done something to Grahame . . . She has *The Book of Beasts*!"

"She found the book?" Flit sipped his tea. "That's wonderful news."

"No! The book itself is magical! We have to go!" He wriggled past and took off down the corridor with George and Flit in tow.

Kenny pounded on Nesbit's closed door. There was no answer. "Grahame! Grahame! Are you in there?" he shouted. George shouldered the door. It swung open to an empty room—except for Nesbit's large spellbook laid open on the floor.

"No one's here." George pulled the sheets back on the bed.

"Is this the bestiary?" Flit walked up to it and flipped through the enormous pages. "It must be. Ah yes, here's an entry on 'Dragons' and . . . huh, that's odd."

"What is it?" asked George.

"Well, there's an entry with *my* name written

on it." He pointed to the writing. "See? It says right here, 'Flit Shrewsbury.'"

As soon as the words left Flit's mouth, there was a whooshing sound. The book slammed shut and he was gone. (Master Flit tells me this looked more painful than it felt.)

"Oh no!" Kenny ran to help, but the book flapped around wildly like a gigantic clam.

George vaulted over the bed, landed on the book, and dug his claws into the leather binding. "Get him out!" The book shook and shuddered under his weight.

Kenny reached for a loosened page, but each time he tried to grab it, the book snapped at him. He scurried around it, looking for a better angle.

"Hurry. I can't hold it much longer," George said with a grunt.

Kenny seized the corner of a page and pried the book open.

"Is he okay?" asked George.

Kenny managed a quick glance. "I don't see him. All I see is a drawing of a big cat named Don-tay."

The covers flipped back open—throwing George and Kenny across the room—and a

guttural roar echoed off the stonework walls.

A beast, larger than a lion, sprang from the pages and landed on the bed. It hissed and raised its scorpion tail.

A screech was heard from above. Nesbit dropped down from the rafters and landed on her book. *"Evanescimus!"* she croaked, and snapped her fingers. She disappeared in a puff of sulfurous vapor, taking the book with her.

"Ew! It smells like rotten eggs." Kenny's nose wrinkled.

A low growl came from the lion creature. A pair of dilated eyes glowed bright in the dissipating smoke.

"Get back, Kenny!" George pushed him aside. "It's a manticore. Very deadly." He drew his sword.

The manticore and George circled the room. Kenny could see the sword's blade wavering in George's grasp. The old knight spoke in a low tone. "I'm gonna cover you to the door, lad. Then I want you to run for help. Understand?"

Kenny could barely hear George over his own heart pounding.

"Do you understand?"

Kenny nodded.

The beast snarled, revealing rows of sharklike teeth. It vaulted over the bed toward the door and blocked Kenny's exit. George slashed at the manticore, but it deftly dodged the attack. Spitting, it swiped back with its massive paw and retractable claws. George parried the blow but stumbled to the floor. While the manticore was occupied in the melee, Kenny bolted to the door. The beast caught sight of him and raised its stinging tail, but before it could strike, the door swung open.

Everyone stopped.

"Dante?" Grahame stood in the doorway, holding a towering stack of pancakes. "Is that you?"

IX. A Conundrum

"Dante. Yes! Yes, that is my name," said the manticore. A spark of recognition flickered in his piercing yellow gaze, and his tail dropped. "Grahame? Do my eyes deceive? Prithee, can it truly be you?"

The dragon rushed up and embraced the manticore. "Forsooth, your eyes do not deceive, old friend! It is I," said Grahame. "How on earth did you arrive?"

"I am not exactly sure. I feel as if I've just awakened from a dream that has gone on far too long." Dante shook his head as if trying to clear his mind.

"You jumped out of Nesbit's book," said Kenny.

"Nesbit! That foul witch placed a cantrip upon me." Dante balled his paw into a fist.

Kenny exchanged looks with George.

"I was in this enchanted place—far from all the hullabaloo going on—but soon I began to forget things, like my name, and lost all desire to do anything except sleep." Dante's face drooped in despair.

"So, there's hope for Flit, then?" said Kenny.

"Wait. What happened to Flit?" asked Grahame.

"It appears that the book somehow traps its victims inside it." George stroked his beard in thought. "Your friend Dante here may have escaped, but Flit has been captured."

Dante jumped at George's voice as if he'd forgotten the knight was there. He slunk behind Grahame, putting the dragon between him and George.

"Oh, my sincerest apologies if I frightened you." George sheathed his sword. "I was unsure of your intent." He held out his paw to shake hands, but the manticore did not reciprocate.

"Goodness, forgive my manners," said Grahame. "Dante, this is Sir George, a most noble knight, if there ever was one, and this"—he patted Kenny's back—"is my dear friend Kenny Rabbit."

The manticore looked him over and said nothing.

Kenny wondered what the manticore was thinking. Seeing yet another living mythical creature was as exciting as meeting a dragon for the first time; however, Grahame had not attacked when Kenny first ventured up to introduce himself.

George broke the awkward silence. "It was young Kenny here who freed you."

"A true advocate for all us *arcane spirits*. Well done, Kenny," said Grahame. "Huzzah!"

Dante bowed his head. "I thank thee, Kenny Rabbit."

There was a clinking of armor coming up the corridor. King Stonehorn stormed into the crowded room, armed guards at his side. "What's going on? I hear there's been a kerfuffle with Nesbit. And where is . . . ? GADZOOKS! Is that a manticore?"

The guards drew their weapons and aimed them at the creature.

"Do not fret, Your Majesty." Grahame pushed away their swords.

"But it's a, it's a . . ."

"He's a friend of Grahame's," said George. "Not to worry. Now sheathe your weapons."

King Stonehorn regarded Dante while Grahame introduced his old friend. "Apologies for your ill welcome," said the king. "We haven't seen a manticore in these parts for ages; however, a friend of Grahame's is a friend of mine."

Grahame bowed. "Thank you, Your Majesty."

"Well, Flit will certainly be happy to have Dante review Nesbit's research. Where is he?"

Kenny and George apprised the king of the morning's events. Dante remained quiet and stood behind Grahame.

"No one kidnaps my subjects—especially a member of my royal staff!" Stonehorn rapped his scepter on the floor for emphasis. He turned to his guards. "Send word to my men-at-arms. Rescue Flit and bring in Nesbit for questioning."

"As you wish, Your Majesty." The guards bowed as they exited. "But we've no idea where she dwells."

"Hmmm." Stonehorn tapped his chin. "That is a conundrum."

"If I may," George spoke up, "I would like to lead the hunt."

"But you've just arrived, Sir George."

"That is true. However, you may recall that I have had some experience in dealing with witchcraft, and, more importantly, I've grown quite fond of Flit."

"Very well, then. It is so," said the king. He placed his paw on George's shoulder. "Godspeed and safe returns. Your wisdom and counsel are needed back here."

"I will, sire. Thank you." George turned to Kenny and Grahame.

"Bid me farewell and smile," said Grahame.

The knight clasped the dragon's hand. "Until we meet again." He spoke to Kenny. "I shall miss you for the time being, but I look forward to

catching up when I visit in the spring."

Kenny hugged his old friend. "Be careful."

"I shall and I will see you lads very soon. Farewell!" With a nod, George was off.

"My men-at-arms shall contain the fugitive, especially with Sir George at the lead," said the king. "But, for the time being, be on alert and steer clear of Nesbit until we learn the extent of her supernatural skills." He walked to the door. "And notify me immediately if you spot her."

"We will, Your Majesty," said Kenny.

"Perhaps we should head back home?" said Grahame.

"Any place that is far from that harridan and her cursed book," added Dante.

"A smart idea," said the king. He shook hands with each of the friends. "Safe journey, Master Kenny." He departed down the corridor, his hooves clacking on the brick floor.

"Why don't we grab some food for the road?" Grahame swung his arm around Dante's shoulder. "It's a long ride and we've got lots to catch up on."

Kenny stood alone in Nesbit's disheveled quarters. As he turned to leave, a small scrap of parchment lying on the floor caught his eye. He picked up the paper to find a list of familiar names jotted down in Nesbit's writing:

Grahame (the dragon)
Sir George E. Badger
Flit Shrewsbury
Kenny Rabbit

Kenny steered his car down the dirt road that led back to Roundbrook. "I mean, Pa dressed as a wizard when we did our performance years ago, but a real-life sorceress? I didn't know they existed. What . . . what if she hunts me down for damaging her book?"

"Old Georgie will find her. Don't you worry," Grahame said as he glided overhead.

"But how does she cast her magic?" The more Kenny thought about it, the more it unsettled him. He gripped the steering wheel tight.

"Conjuration is a long-forgotten art." Dante kept pace alongside the car. "Nesbit is as rare a creature as Grahame and myself."

"But what about—" Kenny was cut off by a loud hissing under the car's hood. The engine clunked repeatedly, then stalled in the middle of the road. "Drat! It's overheated," he said with a sigh, and hopped out. He wrapped his hand with a rag and twisted off the radiator cap. "Grahame, are you sure you installed the new water pump correctly?"

Grahame landed to examine the gasping engine. "Um . . . new water pump?"

"Yeah. You said the problem was a faulty water pump." Kenny stepped back from the radiator as it exhaled a puff of steam.

"It was faulty." Grahame scratched his head. "So . . . I removed it."

Kenny opened the hood to see a welded knot of brass tubing where the water pump had once been. "Oh boy." His shoulders slumped.

"Okay, let me find us some water and we'll get it running. Don't you worry." Grahame flapped his wings and rose high to scan the landscape. "Dante, over there!" He pointed toward a lone hill in the distance. "Is that Castle Gale?"

Dante gazed out at the hill where ruins stood.

A Conundrum

The collapsed walls looked like a crumbling crown on a bald head surrounded by a beard of russet leaves. "Oho! Is that the castle with the spring-fed baths?"

"Yes," replied Grahame. "Where you performed your 'famous' cannonball dive and soaked everyone."

"That was quite a carouse!" Dante snorted. "Remember? You inhaled so much water you couldn't breathe fire . . ."

". . . for a week!" Grahame and Dante finished the sentence in unison. Both of them howled with laughter.

"There should still be water, then. I'll be right back," Grahame said as he flew off.

"Hold on, I'm coming with you." Dante bounded down the road, following Grahame to the ruins.

Kenny frowned and busied himself with the engine until Grahame returned with a mouthful of water. The dragon spit the water inside the radiator and the engine cooled. Kenny cranked up the car. It roared to life, spewing flames from the exhaust.

"Oh, sorry about that," Grahame said with a grin. "My fiery saliva must have mixed with the water in the radiator."

Kenny put the car in gear and sped off, faster than ever. He focused on the road, trying to avoid the ruts while Grahame and Dante reminisced for the remainder of the trip.

By the time they returned home, word had spread of Flit's kidnapping. The evening edition of the newspaper warned of the wicked Nesbit and urged residents to contact authorities immediately should they spot any suspicious activity.

Kenny's parents welcomed Dante into their home but decided it was best that he and Grahame stay hidden in the barn, as opposed to Grahame's cave, on the chance that Nesbit might discover them. "After all," said Kenny's father, "everyone knows where to find the world-famous Roundbrook dragon."

Kenny carried a stack of folded blankets up a ladder to the hayloft, where Dante was licking the inside of an empty pot. "Your mother's carrot stew is delicious. Prithee, thank her for me," he said.

"It's like I told you: you'll not be a starveling while you're here," added Grahame. "Ma Rabbit's meals are as good as anything served in the royal kitchen." He handed Kenny the empty soup pots and took the wool blankets. He draped one over the manticore before wrapping himself. "A chilly autumn evening warmed by a hearty soup . . . This reminds me of the Banquet of—"

"Blackwood!" Dante finished his sentence. "Now, that was a meal for the ages."

Grahame licked his lips. "I can still taste the marzipan cakes."

"Heh." Kenny gave a faint laugh. "Grahame, do you remember when we had the picnic? The one where you got so nervous you . . ." He waited for his friend to finish his thought.

"Oh yes!" Grahame snapped his fingers. "I stepped on Pa's foot."

Dante chuckled to himself.

"You did. Yes." Kenny gestured for him to keep going. "But also, you got nervous and so you . . ."

"Um . . . I ate all the carrots?"

Kenny shook his head.

"Played the piano?"

Kenny sighed.

"Recited poetry? Performed a play?"

"You hiccuped," said Kenny, exasperation in his voice. "You hiccuped and burned off Pa's eyebrows."

"That's right! I do remember." Grahame giggled. "It was just like the time—"

"You sneezed and thus torched the tent at the Meadow Falls Flower Show," said Dante. His giggling made it hard for him to speak. "All because Grahame was allergic to the . . ."

"Snapdragons!" they both said at once.

"Of all things!" Grahame roared with laughter and slapped Dante on the back.

Kenny climbed down the ladder and tromped out the barn door.

X. Glued at the Hip

———⬥———

WITH NESBIT STILL AT LARGE, Grahame and Dante spent the remainder of the week hiding out in the barn. Kenny's chores and homework kept him busy, so much so that he hardly saw his friend.

He finished his work on the farm early Saturday morning. While his mother was at the grocer's, he pulled a cookbook from the kitchen shelf. Thumbing through the pages, he bookmarked a recipe and tucked the book under his arm. The warm midday sun, mixed with a cool breeze, made for pleasant weather as Kenny walked to the barn. Before he reached the open door, the sound of boisterous laughter could be heard coming from the hayloft. Kenny climbed the ladder to find Grahame, Dante, and all twelve of his sisters engaged in a card game.

"Hey!" he said, flourishing the cookbook.

"Good morrow, bantling!" replied Grahame.

"Ready to help me bake dessert for dinner tonight? I'm thinking crème brûlée."

Grahame kept his eyes on his hand of cards. "That sounds tempting, but we're in the middle of this game, so . . . check back later?"

"We're teaching Donty how to play Old Moose," said Kitty.

"It's not Old Moose," said Katherine, giggling. "It's Old Maid."

"No, it's not."

"Yes, it is!"

"Now, kitlings."

Dante discarded a matching pair of cards. "The words printed on the box do say Old Maid, so that is the game we are currently playing."

"Told you!" Katherine stuck out her tongue.

Dante continued. "However, when we are finished, I can teach you Hearts and Stabbers, a card game Grahame and I used to play all the time when we were your age. Doesn't that sound like fun?" The bunnies squealed with excitement.

"Then Kenny can play," said Katy.

"Well, we need an even number of players," said Dante, fanning his cards. "Right now we have fourteen."

"It's okay." Kenny started down the ladder.

"I'll catch up with you later," said Grahame, pulling a card from Dante's hand. "After I win."

Dante laughed. "You won't win. You're terrible at games. Always have been."

Grahame shuffled his hand. "That's because you always cheat! Even when we played with that gaggle of griffins, you . . ."

But Kenny didn't hear the rest. He'd already left.

Dinner that night was a jovial affair, for everyone but Kenny. His parents moved their picnic table into the barn so that they could all sit together. Dante told stories of his childhood and reenacted humorous scenes from his many misadventures with Grahame. The dragon tuned the upright piano and led the family in song after their meal. While Kenny's sisters cleared the table, dessert was prepared, courtesy of Kenny and his mother.

"Now, this is fine dining, indeed!" Grahame thumped the table as the crème brûlée was served, but Kenny said nothing. This did not go unnoticed by Grahame, as he watched him return to the kitchen.

"Don' worry about him, Grahame. He's jus'

bein' moody is all," said Kenny's father through a
mouthful of crème.

Grahame went back to the piano. "Perhaps
a little more entertainment while we enjoy our
dessert?" He tapped several keys and waited until
everyone was seated.

"Sing a song about me," said Kitty.

"Me too!' said the other sisters.

"Well, I have been enjoying a collection of
poetry that George gave me," replied Grahame.

Kenny & the Book of Beasts

"Which has inspired me to write this little verse:

"Me and my friend
went on a trip,
my friend and me,
us two.

"We ate, we shared,
we laughed a lot
at jokes we only knew.

"Though just one day
we had to play
before our trip was through,
I kept a single souvenir,
I cherish it, I do.

"The memory
of all we did
and all we'd hope to do—
a forever treasure
shared by us
of you and me,
us two."

Everyone clapped while Grahame took a bow. His eyes met Kenny's. "And now, for my friend—" Grahame started, but Dante jumped up on top of the piano.

"Hold on, Grahame, I've got one for you." He cleared his throat and shared a piece of poetry about a friendship lasting through the seasons. During the applause afterward, Kenny excused himself from the table.

"Ho, Kenny," Grahame said from the piano. "Do you have a poem you'd like to recite?"

"No," replied Kenny. "I'm good."

A steady drizzle of rain saturated the hills, making them appear like one of Grahame's garish landscape paintings. It was the following weekend and the perfect weather for board games. Kenny's friends arrived just after lunch.

"Long time no see," said Porky upon seeing Charlotte.

"Ha-ha. Sorry I didn't get here sooner," she replied with a yawn. "Rehearsals ran late last night."

Kenny shared the details of his trip to Castle

Stonehorn and Nesbit's arrival (and the kidnapping of poor Master Flit). Both were sworn to secrecy before he introduced them to Dante.

"A manty-core?" Porky said as he followed Kenny to the barn. "Gee willikers, Kinny, you got some neat friends."

"Yeah, well, we've only got room for one more in Parcheesi." Kenny tapped the box under his arm. "Dante won't be able to play, since Grahame is joining us." He swung open the wooden door. The barn was empty.

"Huh. I wonder where they're at," said Charlotte from under her red umbrella.

They're gone. Oh no! Kenny gasped. His mind whirled. "Nesbit!" His heart raced while he searched the sky for the witch on her giant flying book.

"There they are." Porky pointed to the sugar maple across the yard. The friends ran over to Grahame and Dante, who were taking refuge from the wet weather under the tree.

That's the spot where Grahame and I hang out, thought Kenny. As the friends neared, Kenny could hear Grahame and Dante engaged in conversation. They stopped talking and turned at his approach. Dante's shaggy face appeared tear-stained, although Kenny couldn't be sure with the rainy weather. Either way, he didn't care.

"Hey, Grahame, are you ready to play?" he asked.

"Alas, I cannot join you, my friends," replied Grahame.

"But you know it's always better with the four of us." Kenny avoided Dante's gaze. "I'll even let you win."

Grahame gave a soft chuckle. "You'll do fine without me. Dante and I are having a private conversation about some important stuff."

"But you said—"

Dante spoke. "He'll play games with you anon, little one."

Kenny turned around and tramped across the yard through the rain. *Little one?* The words played over and over in Kenny's mind. *LITTLE ONE!*

"Hey, Kinny," called Porky behind him. "What about Parcheesi?"

"Forget it."

———

Charlotte found him in the carriage house, seated behind the wheel of his car. "Everything okay?" She slid into the passenger seat.

He sat silent. Seething.

"I hear you got it running," she said. "I can't wait to go for a ride."

Porky jumped into the backseat behind Kenny. "I bet yer happy Grahame has a creature friend like him now, huh? Take that, archery tent!"

Kenny spoke in a deadpan tone. "Yeah. I'm just thrilled."

"Those two are glued at the hip." Porky watched them through the open door of the carriage house. "They even talk alike."

Dante and I are having a private conversation

about some important stuff, played in Kenny's mind. *Little one.*

"As far as Dante and Grahame know, there are no other manticores or dragons," said Charlotte. "I'd want a friend too, if I were him. Someone who really understands me."

"I understand Grahame." Kenny gripped the steering wheel tight.

"Kenny, he's just catching up with his friend. I mean . . . ," said Charlotte.

Kenny shook his head. "Maybe I'll just leave. Like George did. I'll drive far from here and no one will care."

"That's nonsense," she replied with a playful smile.

"What do you know?"

Charlotte's smile dissolved to a frown and she opened the car door. "Come on, Porky. Let's go."

She walked out into the rain without a backward glance.

XI. The Book of Beasts

WET LEAVES STUCK TO KENNY'S feet and legs as he hiked alone under rain-soaked trees. An orange haze shone through bare branches as the sun sank below leaden clouds. He pulled the collar of his jacket up around his neck to keep warm from the drizzle that remained. A lone katydid chirruped from the bough of a nearby tree, but the creeping frost soon silenced him. "Too cold for music t-t-tonight," Kenny heard him say as he passed.

He arrived at the summit of Shepard's Hill just as dusk blanketed the horizon. The streetlights of Roundbrook flickered in the mist below. Here was the place he'd met Grahame all those summers ago. Here was the place Kenny proved his friendship and loyalty with the help of George, Charlotte, and his parents. . . . But now his parents were busy tending to his sisters, Charlotte was off at another school, George was gone, and Grahame . . . well, thanks to Kenny, he had rediscovered an old friend.

A friend that knew everything about Grahame.

A friend that everybody loved.

A friend that Kenny could not compete with.

He picked up a pinecone and hurled it at the dragon's cave. *It felt good*. He picked up another and another and threw them into the darkness. If he could, he would tear down the amphitheater they'd built.

But then, of course he wouldn't. Not really.

He slumped down on one of the stone benches and put his head in his paws. *Does Grahame miss me at all? Does anybody?*

A flapping was heard overhead. Kenny's ears popped up. He squinted in the rising moonlight but saw nothing. Mixing courage with anger, he called, "Come out, Nesbit! I know you're here." He stood alone. Waiting. A pine tree whispered in the chilled breeze.

"You are as clever as you are handsome, Kenny Rabbit." Nesbit's flying book soared down from the top of Grahame's cave and landed on the leaf-strewn ground. "But I am upset with you." She wagged a finger at him. "You damaged my precious tome and put lives in danger by releasing Dante."

"But . . . but your book ate Flit! I saw it."

"I warned you that it contained ancient, forbidden knowledge." She hobbled toward him, her hunched form leaning heavy on her cane. "Not that it stopped you three thugs from barging into my room. You scared me up to the rafters! That snooping shrew read my sacred tome as if it were a Sunday newspaper. Maybe now he'll be a little less nosy."

"Only because you wrote Grahame's name in there." Kenny pointed at the spellbook with a shaky finger.

"Indeed I did. The king commanded I update the facts, and so I was doing what was asked of me." Her eyes narrowed. "But how would you know that? Were you spying on me?"

Kenny shrank behind the bench he'd been sitting on.

"You care deeply about this dragon, don't you?" asked Nesbit.

"He's my best friend."

"And you're concerned about the well-being of all the other monsters—er, arcane spirits as well?"

Kenny nodded.

"Let me show you something." Nesbit beckoned to *The Book of Beasts*. "*Reclude*." The book's clasps unlocked and the covers swung open. "*Mantichoram mihi ostende*," she whispered. The pages turned on their own, stopping on the entry for "Manticore." The right page was blank, as if Dante's name had been erased, while the left page displayed Nesbit's handwriting and a woodcut illustration of a fuzzy cub with a short, barbed tail. Moving like the animated pages of a flip-book, the trapped manticore cub pawed at the border of its illustration. Nesbit tapped the drawing, and the cub settled, falling fast asleep.

Kenny gasped.

"Do not fret. He is quite safe, as are all the rest." Nesbit waved her hand again and the pages flipped quickly to reveal illustrations of basilisks, cockatrices, chimeras, and the like.

Kenny's eyes opened wide with realization. "They're trapped, just like Dante was. You have to release them!"

"It's not that simple, Kenny. Grahame may be kindhearted, but he's the exception, not the rule." The book slowly closed shut. "Here they can harm no one. And, as I tried to tell the king, these beasts are quite bloodthirsty." Nesbit lifted the hem of her skirt. Her right leg ended in a stump above the ankle. "I lost my foot to a hungry griffin and narrowly escaped with my life." She dropped her skirt. "My apprentice was not so lucky."

A shiver went up Kenny's spine.

"Son, Dante was on the run from the law when I risked my neck to harbor him." Both of Nesbit's eyes were clouded in cataracts; nevertheless, they rested on Kenny. "Ask him how many he's hurt."

"M-maybe I will."

"So then, you know where he's hiding. I know

they're nearby. I can smell them." She sniffed the air. "Tell me where they are and I will safely collect him."

Kenny shook his head and backed away from her.

"This is all one big misunderstanding." Nesbit leafed through the pages of her book to the entry on shrews. Kenny recognized Flit's likeness in one of the detailed illustrations. "I am the good witch here. Not the wicked one King Stonehorn would make me out to be. *Eum libera, Flit Shrewsbury.*" Nesbit reached her hand into the now-glowing illustration. "As a show of my goodwill, you shall see that the royal historian is unharmed." She pulled out Flit and held him by the collar.

He yawned and stretched as if awaking from a slumber. "Master Kenny? Where am I? We're not in the castle."

"It's okay, Flit." Kenny came close.

"That's my name." He let out a sleepy sigh. "I had a dream I'd forgotten it."

"Well, you're safe now."

"Not. So. Fast." Nesbit yanked Flit from Kenny's reach. "If you want to free Flit

Shrewsbury, then listen very carefully." The page began to glow once again as Flit was sucked back into the book. The covers closed while Nesbit continued, "I'll return tomorrow by midday before I depart on my next quest. All you have to do is bring me the manticore. I'll be on my way and things will go back to the way they were before."

The way they were before. Kenny gave the faintest smile at this idea.

"Ah, so that's it." Nesbit's grin revealed dark crooked teeth. "You want things to be less complicated, without a vicious manticore roaming about?"

Kenny shook off his smile. "I have to leave," he said, turning to go.

Nesbit continued talking as he walked away. "Let me guess. Your dragon and the manticore have been together since that rogue escaped. Inseparable. Thick as thieves. Trust me, these creatures care very little of others and only of themselves."

Kenny stopped. "Grahame is not like that."

"Of course not," she cooed.

He paused. "Though sometimes . . ."

"Sometimes?"

The words sprang from Kenny's mouth, as if he had no control. "Sometimes I wish he would do what I want to do, when I want to do it." He put his paw over his mouth. "That . . . that didn't come out right."

"Old Nesbit understands. Why do you think I saved all these poor souls?" She gestured to *The Book of Beasts*. "Stonehorn's kingdom—your home—has remained prosperous and safe for many generations, because of *me*." She kept her gaze on Kenny. "Over the decades I've traveled the globe to make both our worlds safe."

Perhaps Nesbit is just misunderstood after all, thought Kenny.

"Bring me Dante. By tomorrow afternoon your life goes back to normal . . . except you're the celebrated hero who negotiated the rescue of Stonehorn's royal historian."

Is Dante really that vicious? The memory of the snarling cutout beasts at the archery tent

flashed through Kenny's mind. He folded his arms and turned to face Nesbit. "And if I don't?"

Nesbit studied Kenny for a moment, taking her time to answer. "You know, you and I are a lot alike, Kenny." She circled around him, her whiskers twitching. "We understand the importance of preserving these creatures. However, unlike me, you successfully reintroduced a wild dragon into the general populace. I confess: I underestimated you. So, perhaps when I leave tomorrow, it could be with *or without* Dante. The choice is yours."

Kenny blinked in astonishment. He'd done it. He'd stood up to Nesbit. He couldn't wait to tell the others.

"*Avolamus*," Nesbit commanded. The book flapped its covers as it rose from the wet ground, sending up swirls of fallen leaves. "But choose wisely: manticores are easily riled and extremely dangerous. If Dante's bite and claws don't get you, his stinging tail will. There is no antidote for his lethal poison."

"What of Flit?" asked Kenny.

"Do not fret. You've won me over. So I shall release him once I'm in the clear." She climbed atop her flying book. "But, Kenny, no one is to know about our secret pact. If you speak to anyone, they'll come after me and I'll be forced to flee with the historian. And nobody wants that."

Kenny backed up as the book took off.

"Go home, my friend, and sleep on it." The witch soared away, vanishing in the darkness.

XII. A Side We Cannot See

───❦───

THE ORANGE GLOW OF THE FULL moon, glimmering above the trees, lit Kenny's way home. "By tomorrow, Flit will be free and Nesbit will be gone," he said aloud with pride in his voice, but Nesbit's warnings of Dante remained in the back of his mind. He returned to find Grahame and his father setting up his telescope under the star-spattered sky.

"There you are!" Grahame held out his arms to welcome Kenny. "You're just in time. The rain has finally cleared, and you can see the harvest moon in all its glory."

"It's arrived early this year." His father adjusted the knobs on the telescope.

"Where's Dante?" asked Kenny.

"In bed." Grahame pointed to the barn.

"Oh, so you'll hang out with me now because he's not around?"

"That's nonsense." Grahame shooed away Kenny's words. "He turned in early. The poor fellow hasn't been getting much sleep. He's had a lot on his mind."

"Like his past?"

Grahame gave a puzzled look. "Well, yes, but there's more to it than that. It's complicated."

"Hey, come see—" Kenny's father tried to get a word in.

"I bet it's complicated, being on the run and all," said Kenny in a matter-of-fact tone.

"It is, but . . . wait, how do you know about that?"

"Does it matter? It's true, isn't it?"

"Yes . . . but as I said, there is more to it than that." Grahame's brows knit in frustration.

"Why didn't you tell me?"

"Frankly, Kenny, because it's not for me to tell."

"Really? Because I thought—"

"Hold on a minute, boys." Kenny's father stepped in between them. "Kit, come on over here."

Kenny glared at Grahame, then did as he was told. "What?" he snapped.

His father buffed the eyepiece with his handkerchief. "Why doncha take a gander 'n there an' tell me what ya see."

Kenny gave a quick glance into the eyepiece. "It's the moon." He turned to Grahame and started to speak, but his father cut him off again.

"Yup. It is the moon. But tell me: How much of tha moon d'ya see?"

Kenny gave a dramatic sigh and rolled his eyes before looking again. "I see the whole thing. Even the lunar maria."

"That's not true." His father remained calm. "It's only a half moon."

"No, Pa, the moon is full." Kenny pointed at it. "I can see that even without the telescope."

"You really can. It is quite spectacular," added Grahame.

"That it is, Grahame. And it is full," said Kenny's father. "But you're only seeing the

half facing us. There's 'nother half, in complete shadow. A side we cannot see." He put his arm around his son. "The funny thing is, one day you may get to see the other side, when it's revealed."

"I wonder what it looks like," said Grahame.

"Who knows?" replied Kenny's father. "Maybe it's jus' more craters an' crags."

"Or maybe it's more beautiful than what we're looking at right now," said Grahame.

"Until then, all we can do is wonder what secrets it holds," continued his father.

Kenny gazed up as the moon shone down on him. He'd never given much thought to what the other side might look like. Now his mind boggled at the idea. He blinked out of his wonderment to find his father looking at him.

"You good, Kit?"

"Yeah."

"Good. I gotta go say g'night to your sisters." He patted his son's back before walking into the house.

Now alone with Grahame, Kenny spoke first. "I see what Pa is saying and how it relates to Dante . . . but you once told me that some dragons were vicious."

"Some were and some were not. But some knights—just like George—were also vicious. But that was long ago. We are in a much better place now, right?"

Kenny shrugged. "Maybe you're right."

"Of course I'm right. I'm always right!" said Grahame with a grin.

"You are, but . . . I dunno . . . I feel like, since Dante has arrived, you don't want to . . . you know . . . hang out. Just you and me."

"How could you think that?" Grahame knelt down to peer through the telescope. "Besides, what are we doing right now?"

"Yes, but last week we planned to make dessert for everyone, remember?"

"I do." Grahame turned back to him. "And I did want to bake with you, but Dante had just arrived and was still getting acclimated to his new life. I mean, as far as we can tell, he's been gone for over a century. You and I shall prepare the next dessert. Pinkie promise."

"Okay. But—"

"Wait. Pinkie promise," said Grahame, his large pinkie cocked up.

"There." Kenny's pinkie barely wrapped around the tip of Grahame's sickle-shaped claw. "It's just that you and Dante spend so much time together. And with Nesbit on the loose, I'm . . . I'm—" Kenny paused when he heard a deep growling yawn echo from the barn.

"Good evening, fellow astronomers." Dante strolled over to join them. "Have you identified any constellations? Leonis Minoris or perhaps Draco?"

Kenny took a breath. "Dante, do you mind if I finish talking with Grahame?"

"But of course, Kenny Rabbit."

"Alone?"

"As you wish." Dante sauntered back to the barn. His eyes shone bright in the evening shadows.

"So, you were saying?" Grahame returned to the telescope.

"He's still listening," Kenny whispered, pointing from behind his hand.

"No, he's not." Grahame waved him off.

"Yes, I am," replied Dante. "It's okay. We're all friends now, right?"

"That is true, I suppose we are," replied Grahame.

"Argh! Don't you see?"

"See what?" asked Grahame.

Kenny stormed into the house, slamming the front door behind him.

———— ❧ ————

Kenny's father cleared the kitchen table of the empty cereal bowls left by Kenny's rambunctious sisters while his mother poured herself a cup of tea. She sat next to Kenny. "Did you sort everything out with Grahame last night?"

"Not really," he grunted, aimlessly stirring the cold oatmeal in his bowl.

"Listen." She placed her paw on his. "I know there's a lot of transition going on right now, with George moving and Dante staying with us, but—"

"Don't bother." Kenny pushed back his chair and scooped up his bowl. "Pa already had this conversation with me."

"Where are you going?"

"I don't know." Kenny dropped his bowl in the kitchen sink. He shut the back door with a loud bang and tromped out into the yard. Heavy clouds obscured the late-morning sun, but the gray sky did little to dampen the peals of laughter coming from his sisters.

Dante raked fallen leaves underneath the naked branches of the sugar maple while Kenny's sisters jumped in the piles. "My little kitlings," he said, "how is Gam going to be able to burn these if they are not in a single pile? Let's try to keep it nice and tidy. Okay?"

Kenny saw Dante and pivoted toward the carriage house.

"Kenny's here!" Katy squealed and ran to him. She was followed by half her siblings. They skipped around him, throwing leaves and singing, "Kenny's here! Kenny's here! Kenny's here!"

"Okay . . . okay . . . BE QUIET!" Kenny shouted. "I need to be alone."

"Stop yelling!" said Kizzy.

"Yeah," said Katy. "We wanna tell you our secret."

"Secret?" Kenny's annoyance faded.

"Gam's getting flowers," whispered Katy.

"Yeah, for Mama," added Kettie.

"But it's a surprise," continued Kammie. "So don't tell anyone, 'kay?"

Dante joined them. "Grahame wanted to give your mother a break from hosting, so he's picking up lunch and stopping by the florist. He should return shortly."

"That sounds just great," said Kenny in a sarcastic tone, and turned his back to go.

"Kenny, please wait," said Dante. He then addressed the gathered sisters. "My little maidens, perhaps you could give your brother and I a few moments to speak alone?" The bunnies ran off and joined the rest of their clan, frolicking in the leaves.

"What do you want?" said Kenny, not turning to face Dante.

"You dislike me."

Kenny spoke after a moment. "You took my friend away from me."

"Took him?"

"You know what I mean," said Kenny.

"You do not have other friends? Sir George? Charlotte? The hungry porcupine?"

Kenny turned to face him. "I do . . . but they're gone. Besides, Grahame is my *best* friend."

"He is my *only* friend. The only one who understands me."

"Right. Because you're both 'mythical beasts,'" Kenny said with finger quotes.

"*I* am the beast?" Dante said with shock in his voice. "Grahame has tried to help me understand that—even though *you* are the beast, Kenny Rabbit—you and your family are unlike all others."

"Yeah, right!" Kenny began counting off on one paw. "You are the one with a poisonous stinger, a bite with rows of serrated teeth, vicious claws that can shred anything . . . and you're calling *me* the monster? I'm the one who freed you!"

"That you did. And for it I am indebted." Dante remained calm. "But do your words not sting? Is there not a biting tone in how you treat those who care about you? Are you not also capable of vicious things?"

"Who do you think you are? You don't know me!" Kenny pointed an accusatory finger at him. "You've moved in, stolen my best friend from me, and now I'm the bad guy?"

"I did not say that."

"You just said I was!" Kenny threw his arms up in frustration. "Ugh!"

Dante picked a fragment of leaf from his mane, giving the appearance of one hardly interested in Kenny's anger. "You know, for someone so little you certainly ask so much from those you call friends."

"STOP CALLING ME LITTLE!"

Dante barely concealed his snicker. "I don't mean to laugh, but honestly, you are all quite little compared to Grahame and I."

Grahame and I, Grahame and I, Grahame and I.

The words played over and over in Kenny's mind. *He's never gonna leave and it's never gonna be just me and Grahame again.*

Then the idea hit him.

Kenny's voice became eerily calm. Calculated. "If you two are such good friends and I'm such a monster, then, perhaps, you should leave."

"Well," replied Dante, "some time apart may be for the best."

I'll safely collect him. Kenny pointed toward the hill. "Grahame's cave is right up there. Go!"

Dante studied Kenny for a minute. Without another word, he turned and bounded off toward Shepard's Hill.

Kenny's father rolled up on his sheep-drawn cart. His sisters began to fill it with leaves. "Where's he off to?" he asked.

"Wherever." Kenny stomped away, muttering, "I don't know. I don't care."

His father craned his neck, trying to catch a glimpse of Dante through the trees. "He ain't goin' to the top of the hill, is he?"

Kenny shrugged, ignoring the fact that his heart was racing from what he had done.

His father jumped out, seized Kenny by the arm, and spun him around to face him. "Kit, that witch has been seen flyin' around here. Why wouldn't you stop Dante from going up there?"

The reality of Kenny's actions became clear to him as his anger subsided. His eyes grew wide with anxiety and he scanned the overcast sky. There was no giant flying book that he could see. *It's not noon yet. I can get there before she arrives and stop this.* "I have to go!" He wriggled from his father's grasp, raced to the carriage house, and thrust the door open. Grabbing the crank on his car, he tried to start it, huffing with each twist. But the car would not start.

"Pa, what's going on?" His mother stood at the back door, drying her paws on her apron. Kenny's sisters scampered over to her.

"Kenny and Donty got inna fight," said Katherine.

"An' Kenny gave him a time-out in Gam's cave," said Kaye.

His mother collected her daughters. "Okay, well, I am sure the boys can work this out. Come help Mama clean up the leaves."

"Ho, everyone!" Grahame strolled up, holding an armload of groceries and a bouquet of chrysanthemums. "I was just in town and heard news that George and the guard are closing in on our nemesis. Rumor has it that she's been sighted near here. Perhaps we should—"

Kenny didn't hear the rest. He sped out of the carriage house on his bicycle toward the summit of Shepard's Hill.

Puffing with exertion, he pedaled his bike to the topmost stretch, then hopped off and rushed toward Grahame's cave. "Dante! Dante!" Kenny called out. "Where are you?"

There was a flapping overhead as Grahame landed in front of him. "What's going on, Kenny?"

"There's no time." Kenny ran to the entrance of the cave. "Dante! DANTE!"

"Kenny, why is Dante up here? Your sisters said you—"

"Watch out!" Dante leaped from the shadows, pushing Grahame out of the way as Nesbit's large flying book swooped down. She circled around for another attack.

"You!" Grahame inhaled deeply, his nostrils

glowing bright with fiery sparks.

Kenny jumped in front of him. "Don't do it! You'll hurt Flit! You'll hurt them all."

"You'd do well to listen to him," said Nesbit. Her spellbook landed at the cave's entrance. "Dante must return, Grahame. No one is safe while he's here, including him."

"Now, hold on," said Grahame. "You're not taking him anywhere. Let's talk about this. I am sure we can work something out."

"Oh, of course we can work it out," Nesbit purred. "Why don't you join him? *Reclude.*" *The Book of Beasts* rose up. Its great covers opened. Suddenly a large scorpion tail lashed out at Nesbit. She swiftly ducked out of the way as the stinger knocked the book shut.

"Faugh! I missed!" Dante said with a snarl. He poised his barbed tail to strike again.

"Oho! You see, Kenny?" Nesbit clucked. "It is just as I recorded it: a monster always resorts to violence. Nothing has changed. I sheltered this criminal for decades and this is how he repays me."

"You're the monster!" Grahame tried to snatch the spellbook, but it scooted away.

With effort Nesbit hopped back on her book, and it flew up from the ground. "Dante, you told Kenny the truth, right? Of how many you've slaughtered?"

"They were hunting me." Dante swiped at the book with his claws, his hackles raised. "They took my family, my cubs. We'd done nothing wrong. *We simply existed.*"

Nesbit landed in front of the manticore. "Dante, this world still does not want you, most especially Kenny Rabbit."

Dante looked to Kenny for a sign, a signal or gesture that showed Nesbit was lying . . . but the lad looked away, saying nothing. Dante lowered his tail. "If I go, promise you'll leave Grahame alone."

Nesbit nodded. "I will not pursue him. You have my word." She waved her hand. The cover swung open to a blank page and she pulled a quill from her cloak. "*Novum nomen*: *Mantichoras*," she whispered, and wrote the name *Dante*.

"Don't do this. There is another way." Grahame blocked his path.

Dante shook his head. "It is as I told you:

nothing has changed. We are creatures of myth, no longer meant for this world. Farewell, old friend." He pushed Grahame aside and approached the book. "Dante," he read his name aloud. The page began to glow as the manticore was sucked inside. The book snapped shut, then slowly reopened. Dante was gone. A new illustration appeared on the once-blank page.

"He's chosen wisely," said Nesbit. Her eyes darkened as her cataracts faded. A cracking sound came from her back as she stood straight. She gave a sigh of relief, then spoke. "And a deal is a deal. *Flit Shrewsbury mihi ostende.*" The royal historian rolled out from the pages onto a heap of fallen leaves. With a satisfied smirk, Nesbit climbed atop her book with ease. *The Book of Beasts* rose from the ground. "Thank you, Kenny!" she called over her shoulders as she flew away. Under her shadow, Kenny's family rushed up the hillside.

"We heard shouting." There was panic in his mother's voice.

"What's goin' on here?" said Kenny's father.

"A good question indeed." Grahame turned to Kenny. "Tell me you didn't help her."

Kenny could no longer hold in the tears that burned his eyes. "I just . . . I just wanted everything to go back to the way it was before with you and me." He couldn't look at Grahame. He couldn't look at anybody.

Smoke ribboned up from Grahame's nostrils. "You know, I'm starting to think Nesbit is right. Perhaps it is safer within the pages of her book than it is out here with you!"

Kenny's mother started, "Now, hold on, Grahame. Don't you think you're being—" But the beating of his leathery wings drowned out her words as he flapped off after Nesbit.

From the high vantage point atop the hill, Kenny and his family watched Grahame overtake the witch. She cursed and cast spells while the dragon grappled with her giant flying book.

"Oh dear!" cried Kenny's mother.

"Get'er, Grahame!" his father yelled.

"Yeah. Get'er, Gam!" shouted the sisters.

Nesbit called out an incantation and the book rolled in midair. Although Kenny could not make out what she'd said, one word rang clear: *Grahame*.

The book flared bright as Grahame's tail disappeared inside the pages.

Kenny's family gasped.

"Is Gam hurt, Mama?" one of the sisters asked.

With a loud *WHOOSH* the book devoured Grahame, then continued on its flight, disappearing in a heavy fog below the hilltop. Nesbit's triumphant cackle reverberated over the fields below. A bitter wind swept over Shepard's Hill, loosening the last of the faded leaves from the bare trees.

XIII. It's Up to Us

THE RABBIT FAMILY RUSHED HOME. Kenny's father tended to his upset sisters while Flit dashed off a note to the king, apprising him of the situation. The savory scent from a simmering pot of soup did little to soothe everyone's nerves, so Kenny's mother put the kettle on for tea.

"Thank you, Lady Rabbit." Flit blew the steam from his thimble-size mug.

"You're quite welcome. I find chamomile the best remedy for a stressful situation." Kenny's mother poured another cup and handed it to Charlotte. "Thanks for coming right over, sweetie.

He's terribly upset. He won't leave his room."

"I'll see what I can do," said Charlotte, adding a few drops of honey to her drink.

Charlotte knocked softly at Kenny's bedroom door, then entered his room to find him curled up on the floor against the foot of his bed. She sat down next to him. "Hey."

Kenny turned away.

"I brought you some tea."

"I don't want it," he murmured.

Charlotte took a deep breath. "Listen, I know you're upset, but . . . how could you do this?"

He put his head down.

"I mean, you were the first to speak up at the archery tent for Grahame. But as soon as another mythical creature comes along . . . you sell him out?"

"Nesbit knew I would do this. I was jealous. I was a jerk." He spoke to the floor. "I really messed up. Now everyone is gone, Grahame, George . . . even you."

"I'm not *gone*. I'm just going to a different school. What's the big deal?"

Kenny kept his head down. Silent.

"Honestly, Kenny, I don't want to mend clothes all day like my parents." Charlotte set the teacup down. "This school gives me opportunities I didn't have before. It's really important to me. I would think, as one of my best friends, it would be important to you, too. But you never seem that interested."

"That's not true," he mumbled.

"And it's not like I don't want to spend time together. Didn't George tell you I'd want to work at the bookshop with you? Did you accept his offer?"

He shrugged his shoulders.

"Ugh! Kenny Rabbit, sometimes your head is as thick as hickory!" She stood up to leave. "Don't you get it? When we did the play with Grahame and George, I saw what a great performance can do. You inspired me to become something more than I thought I could be. That was your idea. Now everyone in town adores Grahame. That kindness started with *you*."

Kenny looked up at her, his face damp with tears. "I'm sorry."

She knelt down and hugged him.

"I'm so sorry." He clutched her tight. "I didn't mean for this to happen."

"Sometimes things get a little haywire." Charlotte handed Kenny his tea.

He took a sip. "I feel like a runaway car that's gone off the road."

"So, what are you going to do?"

Kenny wiped his eyes. "Grab the steering wheel, I guess?"

Charlotte kissed him on the cheek. "Then grab the steering wheel, Kenny."

Everyone watched Flit walk across a large map that lay atop the kitchen table. Using a pencil, he pointed to a wooded area west of Roundbrook. "When I was contained within her spellbook, I kept dreaming of birch trees as if I were seeing them through a misty window. I believe I was seeing out into her lair, which is hidden somewhere here"—he drew an *X* on the map—"in White Alder Forest."

"Birch trees?" Kenny's father gave a skeptical look. "Sounds like Silverwood t'me."

"Oh yes, of course!" Flit erased his mark and scuttled over to the landmark on the map. "That's the place. I'm confident."

"What will she do now that she has Grahame?" asked Charlotte.

"She mentioned preparing for her next quest," said Kenny.

"Capturing more mythical beasts," added Flit. "Now we know what she's been up to for the last couple of centuries."

"I'd bet she's going to leave the kingdom," said Charlotte.

"And then we'll never find her," groaned Kenny.

Flit removed his glasses and rubbed his eyes. "I fear word may not arrive in time to the king or Sir George."

"I can help with that," said Kenny's mother. "Let me run next door to use the neighbor's telephone. I'll call Ernest."

"Ernest?" asked Flit.

"He's the fastest carrier pigeon in town," replied Kenny's mother, and dashed out the front door.

"Good idea, Ma!" said Kenny. "Grahame said George wasn't far from here."

"But where?" Flit drew a large circle around

Roundbrook on the map. "It's going to take time to locate him, even with a speedy carrier pigeon."

"Then it's up to us to stop her." Kenny stood.

"Hold on, Kit," said his father. "Even on a race-horse you're over a day's travel from Silverwood. Ol' Nesbit could be long gone by then."

"You're right, Pa. But in my car I'll get there in a couple of hours."

His father frowned. "You'll have to keep it runnin' at top speed. If it breaks down . . ."

"I have to try," said Kenny. "It's what a friend would do."

A chilly afternoon breeze swept away the clouds to reveal the bright autumn sun. Kenny led Charlotte across the yard to the carriage house. Flit followed them, speaking quickly.

"Nesbit conjures long-forbidden magic, the kind I've only read about in historic accounts," he said. "I cannot emphasize how dangerous she is."

"I know," replied Kenny as he swung open the carriage house doors. "But I have to help Grahame." He pushed away the fresh memory of his friend being sucked into the book and handed the map to Charlotte.

"So, all we have to do is hold the book open and read Grahame's name to free him?" she said.

"I believe so," said Flit. "But it won't be easy. You're going to have to do it without her finding out; otherwise, you may end up trapped as I was."

"How are we going to do that?" Charlotte tossed her handbag into the car and slid into the front seat.

"I dunno," said Kenny. "But I think she draws power from the creatures once they're trapped in the book."

"Hmmm. Interesting theory." Flit cleaned his glasses with a handkerchief.

"I don't think it's a theory." Kenny put on his driving goggles. "She seemed refreshed . . . healthier . . . after Dante was sucked in."

"Well, that would explain her longevity."

"Sounds like we've got our work cut out for us." Charlotte buttoned up her coat.

"Don't worry," said Kenny. "We'll figure it out on the way." He turned the starting crank twice and the car grumbled to life.

It's Up to Us

Ernest, the carrier pigeon, landed in the yard in front of them. "Just try to stall her," Flit said. "In the meantime, I'll locate Sir George and we'll rendezvous with you as soon as we can." He hurried toward the wicker passenger basket held in Ernest's claws. "Good luck, Master Kenny and Lady Charlotte." Flit waved as Ernest took off and soared away from Old Rabbit Farm.

Kenny hopped behind the wheel and adjusted his cap and goggles. "Ready?"

"Ready," replied Charlotte.

Kenny waved to his family as he sped off.

"Bye-bye!" his sisters called after him. "Bring back Gam and Donty."

The car rumbled at full speed. Kenny gripped the wheel tight, hoping that they would make it in time.

"It seems like there is only one road through Silverwood." Charlotte studied the map as it flapped in the breeze. "You're gonna see a left turn leading to Dunhill. It should be coming up any minute . . . right here!" She pointed at a small hand-painted sign hanging by a nail.

Kenny swerved the car and raced toward the forest looming ahead.

"Slow down," Charlotte told him. She stood in her seat, searching the area as they chugged down the dirt road.

"There're birch trees everywhere," said Kenny.

"I know." Charlotte sat down, returning to the map. "How are we going to find her?"

Kenny recalled everything he knew about Nesbit, hoping for a clue. Her magical abilities seemed to know no end. She flew on a book that could trap anyone she liked, and she could disappear in a puff of smoke. A whiff of sulfur wafted past. Kenny slammed on the brakes. The car skidded to a stop. "Do you smell that?"

Charlotte sniffed the air. "Gross! Rotten eggs!"

"Exactly! Where is it coming from?" Kenny scanned their surroundings.

Charlotte pointed. "Hey, there's smoke over there. D'ya see it?"

"Oh, I see it." A satisfied smile drew across Kenny's face, and he steered his car in the direction Charlotte had indicated. They parked in a glade just off the road, not far from the source of the smoke.

"So how do we stall her?" Charlotte spoke softly as she followed Kenny on foot.

"We don't," replied Kenny. "We rescue Grahame . . . and Dante, too, if he'll come."

"Are you sure about that?" she asked. "You heard what Flit said."

"I know, but I've got to make this right," replied Kenny. He stopped and listened to the mournful sound of the wind rattling the leafless trees.

The gust blew away the smoky haze to reveal a gigantic ancient birch at the center of a copse. Its barren branches and paper-white bark gave it a ghostly appearance. Mysterious mushrooms and other bizarre fungi sprouted from its crackled column while bone wind chimes tinkled in the branches above. Perched in the fork of the trunk was a ramshackle cottage with frayed rope bridges leading in and out, like a giant spiderweb.

Kenny put his finger to his mouth and stepped on the nearest bridge. It swung and swayed, causing him to lose his footing and slip off. He

tried again but fell, landing on his back.

"Are you okay?" Charlotte whispered.

"Yeah, I'm fine," he replied, frustrated. "I'm a hopper, not a climber."

"You can say that again." She pulled off her shoes. "Stay here. Let me figure out the best way up." In several graceful bounds she was at the front porch. She peeked through the leaded windows before silently returning.

"Is . . . is she in there?" asked Kenny.

"Yeah. She was drawing a weird circle with strange symbols on the floor and placing candles around it." Charlotte tested her footing on one of the bridges. "Okay, this way. Follow me."

Kenny stayed close to Charlotte and clambered up to the cottage. They crouched behind stacks of junk heaped on the front porch. From inside came a scraping sound, as if heavy objects were being moved. Kenny and Charlotte snuck a glance through a missing pane of the porch window.

A spry Nesbit shoved an upholstered chair into the corner of her cluttered parlor. "Just . . . a little . . . more . . . room," she said with a grunt. She knelt down, holding a piece of chalk, and finished drawing the magic circle on the floor. Lighting candles, she chanted, "Time for a doorway to a place far from Stonehorn's troublemakers, *ianuam reclude*." The floorboards in the center of the circle vanished, but instead of creating a hole to the ground below, it revealed a dark magical vortex. Nesbit grabbed a teacup and dropped it into the vortex. She waited, hand cupped to her ear, but no sound of breaking china came.

"Perfect," she said, and tossed more belongings in the portal. As she passed *The Book of Beasts*, she stroked its trembling cover. "Don't fret, my pets, you're coming too." It settled in response to her words, remaining at its place on an oversize bookstand.

While Charlotte kept watch, Kenny slid down and out of sight. "What was I thinking? This is hopeless." Fear fluttered inside him like a trapped butterfly.

"Hey, look!" Charlotte tapped him on the shoulder. "She's going upstairs."

Kenny turned back but only caught a glimpse of Nesbit's scaly tail sliding up the rickety staircase.

"Now's our chance. We have to go!" whispered Charlotte.

It's Up to Us

Kenny took a deep breath. *You can do this.* Focused, he opened the door and slipped inside with Charlotte close behind. No sooner had they entered the cottage than the spellbook flapped its pages in agitation, like a bird disturbed. Kenny pointed to the open metal clasp on the book's cover. "Quick! Close it or it'll attack."

Charlotte leaped over the portal, landed on the book, and secured the clasp in one deft move. It clicked as it fastened shut.

Kenny gave a sigh of relief. Keeping an ear focused on Nesbit, who was still upstairs gathering her things, he skirted the edge of the swirling portal to join Charlotte at the book. "Okay. Let's grab it and get out of here," he whispered.

It's Up to Us

They lifted the large, heavy tome from its stand and quietly shuffled toward the open door. The book jerked about, trying to break free, but they held it tight. As they neared the doorway, Charlotte stopped.

"What is it?" asked Kenny in a high-pitched whisper. The sweat on his palms caused the book to become slippery in his grasp.

"The door's not big enough," Charlotte said in a low voice, struggling to keep her grip as well. "How does she even get it in here?"

"We have to . . . oof . . . turn it on its side," replied Kenny. "We'll do it on three, okay? One . . . two . . ."

"Eldritch Nesbit!" a stern but familiar voice called from outside. "Under orders of His Majesty, King Stonehorn, I command you to surrender. You are surrounded." Kenny glanced out the door to see George seated on his mount, reading from a proclamation. A squad of men-at-arms circled the tree, some carrying torches, others with swords and bows drawn.

"So much for being stealthy," Kenny grumbled.

"Kenny, behind you!" yelled Charlotte.

XIV. The Stuff of Myth and Legend

"THIEVES!" NESBIT SHRIEKED AS she scrambled down the stairs. "You've messed with the wrong witch, Kenny Rabbit!" She picked up a flickering crimson candle and blew on it. A fireball spewed from her mouth.

Kenny and Charlotte shoved the book out the door. It tumbled to the ground below and landed with a loud thud. They jumped from the porch as flames erupted from the doorway behind them.

"Kenny, my boy!" George trotted to him on his steed. "You found the spellbook. Well done!"

"Indeed!" added Flit, seated in front of

George. "Have you rescued Grahame?"

"Not yet." Charlotte helped Kenny to his feet.

"Stall her," said Kenny, panting. He and Charlotte lifted the book and began lugging it to the car.

"Fear not! We shall prevail!" George raised his sword. "We are armed with hagstones, magic mirrors, and other protective charms." He circled the witch's tree and shouted orders.

Nesbit's voice cut through the still of the forest, casting curses and hexes. Her screeches were mixed with the yelling of the soldiers and the clanging of steel weapons. Huffing from exertion, Kenny and Charlotte made it to the open glade at last.

"Let's lean it here, against these trees," said Kenny, and they set the book down. "And whatever you do, don't open it."

"You don't have to tell me twice." Charlotte stooped over to catch her breath. "So, what now?"

Kenny rubbed his forehead in thought. "Once we open that clasp, this thing is gonna buck around like crazy. Even George had a hard time holding it down. We need to secure it somehow."

Charlotte studied the straps and stitchery that wrapped around the spellbook's spine, holding it together. "Got any rope?"

"I do!" Kenny ran to his car and flung open the door; he returned with a coil of rope. Slinging the coil over her shoulders, Charlotte handed the frayed end to Kenny.

"Help me tie it down," she said.

Kenny did as he was told. In minutes, they'd snaked the rope through the straps that reinforced the spellbook's binding and anchored it to several nearby trees.

Far in the distance, more yelling came from Nesbit's lair. Something exploded.

"That didn't sound good." Kenny's stomach churned. He tested the knot tied around the tree trunk. "This is nice and tight."

"It's a slipknot," Charlotte replied as she gathered the last of the rope. "I learned it in sewing class . . . you know, at my school that you don't like?"

"Aw, c'mon, Char—" he started.

"I'm just messing with you." She winked at him.

He smiled back as he reached for the clasp. "As soon as I open it, tie off the cover so it can't shut, okay?"

Charlotte nodded and readied herself, rope in hand.

"Uh-oh," said Kenny.

"Uh-oh, what?"

Kenny wrestled with the clasp. "It's locked tight. I can't open it." A chilly wind snaked through the wood, but his brow was damp with sweat. There was a scuttling sound coming from behind them. Kenny turned with a start.

Flit emerged from the wood, his jacket scorched in places and the tip of his tail smoking. "Any luck?" he asked.

Kenny shook his head. "I can't open the book. It's magically locked."

"You best do something quick, Master Kenny! I don't know how much longer Sir George and his men can hold her off." *BOOM!* They jumped at the sound. Flit ran back toward the battle. "I'm off to help. HURRY!"

Kenny tugged his ears in frustration. *I have the spellbook but no way to get Grahame out, and all*

I have to do is read his name. Then it hit him all at once. He thought of the scrap of paper he'd found in Nesbit's quarters. "My name is in the book."

"Kenny? What are you saying?" Charlotte spoke fast, her eyes wide. *The Book of Beasts* thrashed and thumped at its binds.

Kenny paced, trying to figure it out. "But it can't suck me in, because it's locked . . . and only Nesbit knows the spell to open it. But if my name is already written in there—"

"What does the book do when you read your name?" interrupted Charlotte.

"It creates a portal, a doorway to the place where Flit was. Where Grahame is."

"And all she does is write your name in the book?"

Kenny nodded.

Charlotte dashed to the car, grabbed her satchel, and pulled out a fountain pen.

"Yes!" said Kenny as he realized what she was planning.

Charlotte wrote his name on the cover of the book, adding a decorative flourish. As soon as she did, the writing began to glow. Through the

wood, the fighting at Nesbit's lair became louder. "We're running out of time," she said. "You're gonna have to be quick."

"No, I need to be fast. *Really fast*." Kenny rolled up his sleeves and ran to the car. He started it in one crank, hopped in, and revved the engine.

"Where are you going?" said Charlotte.

"Give me ten minutes." He threw the car in reverse and backed it up, giving him ample space. "If this works, the book is going to open up and suck me in. When it does, keep it on my page, no matter what. If it closes, I'm done for."

"I'll try." Charlotte readied herself. "Be careful, okay?"

Kenny nodded and rammed the throttle up. The wheels peeled out and the car careened across the glade, straight toward the book. Right before it crashed, he read his name aloud, "Kenny Rabbit."

There was a flash.

A vast sunlit field, overgrown with wildflowers, spread out in a valley across the horizon. In the distance a rainbow shimmered over a waterfall cascading down from emerald-green hills. A blue-bird's song chittered on the breeze. Kenny's car skidded to a stop and he hopped out.

"It's beautiful," he said, inhaling the sweet-scented air. Immediately the anxiety of rescuing his friend left him. His eyelids became heavy, as if he were fighting off a nap. He leaned against the side of his idling car, watching a butterfly dance around his smiling face. His words began to slur. "I could just stay . . . here . . . forever."

BANG!

The car backfired, waking the rabbit with a start. He shook his head as the magical effects of the book began to dissipate from his mind.

A shaggy head popped up from a nearby field of wildflowers. It let out a yawn, and the rabbit could see every row of razor-sharp teeth in its mouth. The shaggy creature blinked as he focused on his surroundings.

"I know you." The rabbit walked toward the shaggy creature. It was the manticore.

"And I know you," he replied.

"But I can't remember your name." The rabbit's face furrowed in concentration. He could

recall the names of his family and friends back
home, but his own name escaped him.

"Don't bother," said the manticore. "Like you,
I lost it when I entered this place."

Memories floated back into the rabbit's mind.
He spoke fast. "I'm sorry for everything I did. If
we hurry, we can escape."

The manticore turned away and lay down to
resume his nap. "I am glad you recognize your
hurtful behavior, but you're too late. Farewell. Go
back to the safety of your world."

"It's not my world; it's *our* world," replied the

rabbit. "Nobody should be kept in here. I can get you out."

"You've betrayed me, just like all the rest. Why should I trust you?" The manticore kept his back to him.

The rabbit spoke softly. "You were right. I am capable of vicious things. But I didn't dislike you because of *who* you were. I just thought you were taking my best friend away from me. You both have so much in common. That was hard for me. Now I see the truth."

"And what is the truth?" The manticore turned to face him.

"Friend or monster," replied the rabbit. "Each of us has to decide who we're going to be."

"And what have you decided?"

The rabbit shrugged his shoulders. "I am somewhere in between, trying to change for the better. That's not always easy to do."

The manticore studied him for a moment before speaking. "I accept your apology. But you cannot apologize for the rest of your kind. They will hunt me, just as they did before." He lay back down. "I'm better off here . . . in this purgatory."

"No one will bother you, or any of the others in here," said the rabbit. "King Stonehorn would see to that. He cares about all the creatures in his kingdom. Didn't he say a friend of yours is a friend of mine?"

The manticore looked the rabbit in the eye. "You are naive. Unlike our dragon friend, there are dangerous beasts trapped within these pages. What of them?"

"It's not up to me. Let them choose their own destiny," said the rabbit.

The manticore raised an eyebrow at this reply.

"I don't know. Maybe they just need a friend, like all of us," continued the rabbit.

The manticore scratched his chin in thought, which reminded the rabbit of the dragon. There was a sound of distant thunder. The landscape quaked.

"We have to go. Gather as many as you can, including our dragon friend," said the rabbit. "You have to trust me."

The manticore stood. "Okay, rabbit. I shall help you do this. But I do not know where our dragon friend is, so we're going to need time."

The Stuff of Myth and Legend

Thunder rumbled. The landscape shook. A flurry of butterflies flew across the field toward a glowing doorway. They entered the doorway, vanishing in the light.

"The exit!" said the rabbit.

"It remains open?" asked the manticore.

"Yes, Charlotte is keeping it open." The rabbit smiled when he said her name. Thunder grumbled over them.

"What is going on out there?" asked the manticore.

"We . . . uh . . . maybe swiped the book."

The manticore looked up at the blue cloudless sky as a thunderclap reverberated across the valley. "And Nesbit is angry."

The rabbit gulped. "You could say that."

⁓❧⁓

Charlotte strained against the force of the book as she pulled the rope, now threaded through the clasp, and tied it off to a tree. The covers wriggled and twitched in their binds, trying to shut, but the book remained open.

"Oh, hurry up!" She bit her nails while she

watched the animated illustration of Kenny speaking with Dante but could not hear a word they said. What she could hear was the battle intensifying and drawing close to the glade.

"We've got'er now, boys!" George's voice rang through the wood.

The cupola of Nesbit's cottage blew off in a burst of sparks and purplish smoke. Moments later, a kaleidoscope of butterflies flew from the pages of the spellbook, fluttering around Charlotte.

<hr />

The rabbit hopped into his car while the large manticore tried to sit in the backseat.

"Can't you get in?" asked the rabbit.

"Not really," said the struggling manticore. "I told you that . . . oof . . . you're all little to me."

The rabbit smiled at this.

The manticore seized the seat with its claws, ripped it out of the car, and threw it into the field. Sliding behind the driver's seat, he fit snugly in the back.

"Okay," said the rabbit. "Lead the way."

"Very well." The manticore pointed and they sped off.

⌖

"Lady Charlotte." Flit ran from the underbrush, covered in ash, his whiskers singed. *(Master Flit tells me they took forever to grow back.)* "Any luck?"

George rushed up behind him. "Where's Ke—"

"Don't say his name!" Charlotte clamped her paw over his mouth. "He's inside the book with the manticore. They're trying to rescue you-know-who. They just left in his car."

Flit's tiny eyes grew wide with surprise. "He's in the book?"

"With the motorcar?" asked George.

"Oh, this is not good." Flit wrung his hands. "Not good at all."

"Why?" asked Charlotte.

"Because," said George. "Nesbit gave us the slip."

"What!" squeaked Charlotte. Her eyes darted back and forth, scanning the nearby wood.

"We thought we had her, sire," said one of

the armored soldiers, entering the glade. He was followed by the rest of the squad. It was clear there were fewer present than when they'd first arrived.

George shook his head. "I know. She 'played dead' on us."

"Oldest trick in the book," added Flit.

"And we fell for it," continued George. He gripped his sword tight. "Men, ready your weapons. Protect the book at all costs until my squire has escaped."

The Stuff of Myth and Legend

A-HOO-ga! A-HOO-ga! The rabbit honked his horn repeatedly while his car zoomed past fields, through brooks, and over grassy knolls. A stampede of now-awakened mythical creatures joined them. Majestic unicorns, growling chimeras, and others galloped alongside the car, while feathered griffins, hippogriffs, and a Pegasus flocked overhead. Seated next to the rabbit was an Al-mi'raj with its long, slender horn pointing up to the cloudless sky. A fuzzy manticore cub nuzzled the large, older manticore seated behind the rabbit.

"We're almost to the exit," the rabbit announced over the whine of the engine. "It's just up ahead."

"There is still no sign of our dragon friend," said the manticore.

"Don't worry. We'll find him." The rabbit raced onward.

"Filthy thieves! You'll pay dearly. I'll turn you to flies and devour you all." Nesbit swooped down on a flying broom. Charlotte and Flit jumped out of her way and hid behind the covers of the open spellbook.

"Take aim, lads, and don't let her near the book!" shouted George.

Nesbit opened a velvet pouch full of acorns, each with an arcane glyph scratched on its shell. She plucked one out. "*Igni!*" she said. The acorn burst into purple flames, and she hurled it at George. The old knight pulled an ornate hand mirror from his belt and whacked the flaming acorn like a tennis ball. It zipped past Nesbit's head.

"Nice try!" She lobbed a volley of acorns down at George, but he dodged them all; however, one struck a soldier. Upon hitting him, the flame consumed his body, transforming his patinated armor to exoskeleton. It extinguished with a puff to reveal a large greenbottle fly buzzing around in confusion. "Another down!" Nesbit cackled in triumph. She flew past the open book, her eyes scanning Kenny's name written on the open page. "Perfect," she continued, laughing. "Just too good to be true!"

"I think we should get our friend out of there," said Flit. "We're running out of soldiers."

"Not yet," replied Charlotte. "Let's give him a little more time."

Zooming over them, Nesbit yelled, "Stay put, little maggots. You're next!"

By the time the rabbit skidded to a stop, the radiator was whistling like an angry teakettle. "Okay, here's the exit."

The menagerie of mythical creatures gathered around the glowing doorway, but none dared enter.

"Go ahead." The rabbit shut off his car and pointed to the door. "You're free. That's the way out."

A scaly amphisbaena peered through the doorway. "Perhaps we should think this through," he said. His second head nodded in agreement.

"Indeed. Who knows what awaits us out there?" A ring-necked wyvern landed near the door. "I remember being chased by knights."

"My friends." The manticore stood in the middle of the gathering. "It is not the hateful world we left long ago. Trust me. Trust my rabbit friend."

"I'm not so sure," murmured a unicorn, flicking back her flowing mane. "Here, we're safe from danger."

"And it is comfortable," said a red-tailed griffin. "Even if we're penned in. There is no pain. No suffering."

"Life is not always sunshine and napping," said the rabbit. "You've forgotten how to live."

"Don't you want the freedom to go about and do as you wish?" asked the manticore. "With new friends?"

"Sure," said the griffin. "But it will be different from the life we've grown so used to. We're with our kind. Look how many of us are in here. Maybe that's how it should be."

"But times have changed." The rabbit joined the manticore. "You'll be received with open arms. You're magic. The world is richer with you in it. You'll be celebrated. Folks haven't seen you all in so long that you're considered the stuff of myth and legend."

"So why change it now?" asked a hippogriff.

"Because sometimes good can come from change," said the rabbit.

"If you've wanted to break free from this zoo that Nesbit's trapped us in, now's our chance," said the manticore. "Come. Follow me!" He leaped through the doorway. The assembled creatures watched.

Then the unicorn jumped through, then the hippogriff, followed by the chimera.

The entire herd followed.

"Wait!" the rabbit called. "Where's the dragon?"

Nesbit swooshed down on her broom and barreled toward George. Flanked by his remaining guards with their weapons drawn, he held his ground in front of *The Book of Beasts*.

The witch thrust her paw into her velvet pouch. "Now, shoo fly, shoo!" she said, pulling out a handful of fiery acorns.

Dante bounded out of the book, followed by every prisoner that had been trapped inside. George and company scattered out of the way as creatures jumped, flapped, slithered, and ran in all directions.

"NO!" screamed Nesbit. "How could you have gotten out? Do not abandon me. I gave you the perfect sanctuary. COME BACK!"

Among the last to approach the exit from the bestiary was a lone field cricket. He sprang past the rabbit, still inside the book frantically trying to start his car.

"Thanks for helping us critters outta here." The cricket tipped his hat.

"You're welcome," replied the rabbit, and turned the starter crank. The car hacked up a cloud of smoke but did not start.

"Need a hand?" the cricket said in a jovial manner. "I've got a few to spare."

The rabbit stopped and wiped his brow. "I'm trying to get my car started so I can find my dragon friend and get out of here."

"Dragon? A blue fellow about yay tall?" The cricket stretched to his full height, which was about an inch.

The rabbit chuckled despite the situation. "Yeah . . . WAIT! Do you know where he is?"

"Right over there. Under that weepin' willow tree."

"Thanks!" The rabbit dashed toward the tree. He slipped through the veil of leaves to find his friend snoring in the shade.

"Wake up! Wake up!" The rabbit jostled him. "We've gotta go."

"You . . . you're here! Am I dreaming?" Still half-asleep, the dragon hugged the rabbit tight. "I'm so sorry. I've been such a cad."

"It wasn't your fault. It was mine. I put you in this mess," said the rabbit. "I am the one who is sorry."

"No, it was me. It had been so long since I'd seen Dante."

Dante. Yes, that was the manticore's name, thought the rabbit. "I know, I know." He took the dragon by the hand. "Can we continue this later? After we're out of the book?"

"Yes. But I want you to know you are my *best* friend." The dragon handed the rabbit a folded piece of paper. Written on it was the poem the dragon had recited at dinner.

The rabbit stopped. "I thought you wanted to be friends with Dante instead of me."

"Come now. That's silly," said the dragon with a yawn. "Besides, you have other friends, right? Like George?"

"Yes."

"And Charlotte?"

"Of course."

"And Porky and Polly?"

"Well, yeah . . . I guess," replied the rabbit.

"My point is you are surrounded by friends. One doesn't replace another."

"You're right," said the rabbit, pushing the dragon toward the car.

"Friends may come and go, but George, Charlotte, and me—we'll always be there for you."

The sulfurous smoke from Nesbit's spells cleared to reveal her spellbook still tied down to several trees in the empty glade. A lone cricket hopped from its open page and landed in the leaf clutter.

"We need to call him out now." Flit ran toward the front of the open book.

"No!" Charlotte pulled him back. "He hasn't rescued the dragon yet."

"Come out, come out, my little maggots. Time to spread your wings as fat little flies."

Flit and Charlotte peeked out from behind the book's cover.

George was on his knees at the far end of the glade. Nesbit was standing next to him, her broken broom at her feet. She was now decrepit: Her eyes were a ghostly white. Her voice wheezed as she spoke. "Give me my book." She held a flaming acorn in her shaky claws, just inches from

George's head. "If you do not act quickly, your gallant knight becomes a cowardly blowfly."

"Okay, okay." Flit walked out with paws raised. Charlotte followed.

"Just don't hurt him," she said.

"I make the commands here," said Nesbit with a sneer. "And I command you to untie my book. NOW!"

<hr />

". . . And furthermore," said the dragon as he followed the rabbit to the doorway, "Dante may be an old friend, but you, my dear bantling, are my very best friend. So you see—"

"Please." The rabbit got into his car. "Let's just get out of here."

"Silly me. Of course," said the dragon. He bent over and turned the car's starting crank. The engine coughed and wheezed as it started. "What have you been doing to this thing?" He grimaced as exhaust billowed around him. "It sounds terrible."

"I've been rescuing all of your friends."

"Oh yes, well . . . don't worry. We're going

to fix your car right up as soon as we get home. Okay, best friend?"

"Okay, okay." The rabbit pointed to the door. "Can we just go?"

"All right, all right." The dragon paused. "Boy, oh boy, I can't wait to see the look on Link's face when we all show up at the archery tent during next year's Harvest Festival."

"Please!" pleaded the rabbit.

The dragon struck a pose. "See you on the other side," he said as he pirouetted through the doorway.

And, in a blink, the doorway disappeared, leaving the rabbit inside.

"Ta-da!" Grahame landed his pirouette in an open glade and took a bow. He stood to see Charlotte, Flit, and George tied to a large birch tree, pointing behind him. Spinning around, Grahame saw Nesbit in front of her spellbook, the flaming acorn still clutched in her hand.

"*Clude*," she whispered. The book slammed shut. Its clasp locked. "It's fitting that the one who has undone the collection of my life's work is the only one left in my book. What delightful plans I have in store for our troublesome friend."

Charlotte raised her voice. "You mean Kenny Rabbit!"

"You said his name. Good try," the ancient Nesbit croaked with glee. "But it won't work." She pointed to Kenny's written name, now smudged on the cover.

"Let him go!" Grahame's eyes blazed.

"Oh, I will." Nesbit chortled as she slowly climbed onto the book. "But first I'll put him on the shelf. After about a century, my pain, caused from his misdeeds, should subside and I'll release him. Of course, by then everyone he's ever cared about will be long gone. But that's the price you pay."

"Not if we can help it." Dante stepped out from the wood, his tail poised to strike. Mythical beasts of every sort joined him and surrounded the witch.

"*Evanescimus!*" Nesbit snapped her fingers to disappear . . . but nothing happened.

"You've lost your powers," said Dante as he moved in. "You're an aging whiffet. Your bag of tricks, empty."

"Not entirely," said Nesbit. She held up the flaming acorn. "Move one step closer and Kenny is gone forever."

"You wouldn't dare burn your own book," said Grahame.

"Try me." She moved the flame next to a loosened page poking out from the binding. It sparked and began to burn.

The rabbit collapsed in his seat, blinking in disbelief at the space where the doorway once was. *Nesbit retrieved her book*, he thought. *I hope the rest are safe out there.*

He turned his car around and drove across the field toward the shimmering rainbow. *I'm never getting out.* Despite the time he knew he'd spent inside the book, it seemed as if not a minute had passed in the artificial world. The bright sky remained cloudless. The wildflowers dipped and bobbed in a spring breeze just as they had when he first arrived.

Cursed, Dante had said. The rabbit drove through the silent field where birds had sung, crickets had chirped, and manticores had roared. Now the landscape was abandoned. He had been so fearful of his friends leaving. In the end, it was he who had left them, forever trapped in a book while their lives went on without him.

Never again would he see Grahame torch crème brûlée with flame from his nose; nor would he be able to challenge George at the chessboard. He would no longer be able to talk about his favorite books with Charlotte or hear the laughter of his sisters playing in the backyard. The rabbit's thoughts drifted to his parents. There would be no more spoons to lick from his mother's baking or listening to his father's tales about this and that, especially those "blasted automobiles." He laughed to himself when he thought of Pa's story of a car blowing up in town. He would miss his jokes and . . . WAIT.

The rabbit wheeled the car around and raced toward the spot where the doorway had been. A stream of boiling water hissed from the radiator, spraying on the windshield. He adjusted his goggles and pushed the gas throttle to its limit. The engine roared in protest. In seconds there would be no more water to cool the engine, water that had been mixed with Grahame's fiery saliva.

The engine choked.

The car exploded.

The Book of Beasts blew open. Its singed pages drifted down like giant leaves scattered in the wind. Kenny Rabbit coughed and sat up. He was in the middle of the glade, holding the steering wheel of his car.

"I'll kill you!" Nesbit shrieked. "I am Eldritch Nesbit and you—"

Grahame picked her up, threw her into the glowing spellbook, and slammed it shut. He held

it firmly even though it shuddered in his grasp.

"Lock the clasps!" said Kenny.

"I can't." Grahame struggled to hold the covers shut. "They're . . . broken from . . . the explosion."

"She's going to break free!" cried Charlotte.

"No, she's not," said Dante. His tail struck the cover in a flash, impaling the entire book with a long, barbed stinger. He snapped the stinger from his tail where it remained in the book, holding it shut.

Kenny stood with the aid of George and Charlotte and limped over to the book. "How'd you get her in there?"

"It was open to the title page." Grahame had a self-satisfied grin on his face. "Everybody knows the author is always listed on the title page. She said her name and I seized the moment. *Carpe diem!*"

"*Carpe diem*, indeed, my good friend," said George. "That was quick thinking."

"Now that she's trapped in there, should we let it burn?" asked Flit.

"Burn it?" Grahame snuffed out the flame

dancing on the corner of the cover. "What sort of unchancy firedrake do you think I am? I'd just as soon burn my tail than burn a book . . . even a grimoire such as this."

"She has what she desired." Dante licked the stump on his tail. "She is now safe from all the dangerous beasts of this world."

"Yup," added Kenny. "Every one of us."

XV. The King's Peace

⸻❦⸻

THE FOLLOWING WEEK, KENNY found himself back at Castle Stonehorn with his friends and family. Dressed in their finest clothes, they stood with members of the royal court, local villagers, and other travelers from far and wide, gathered at the back gates of the castle.

Queen Stonehorn addressed the assembly. "Welcome to the royal sanctuary." She opened her arms to acres of pristine forest that stretched beyond the castle grounds, as far as the eye could see. "Please join me in welcoming our special guests."

The crowd clapped as King Stonehorn led the procession. A magnificent herd of mythical creatures marched through the castle courtyard and crowded around the king and queen. "My new friends, it is with great honor that we celebrate you on this day. Here at Stonehorn Sanctuary you may come and go as you please," said the king.

"And regardless of wherever you may travel, you shall remain protected under the King's Peace," added the queen.

"Do let us know if we can be of any further help," said the king. "Well . . . off you go!"

The crowd clapped and cheered as the herd dispersed. Some creatures frolicked near the

castle, while others took wing and left.

"I thank thee, Your Majesty," said Dante. "For giving us a second chance."

"We all make mistakes." Stonehorn clasped Dante's paw. "Even kings."

"Speaking of mistakes, what of Nesbit and her book?" asked George.

"Filed away." Flit dusted off his paws. "In the library's special collection . . . or was it the dungeon? I can never remember."

King Stonehorn gave a belly laugh at this. He turned to Kenny. "So, lad, are you up for completely rewriting the new edition of *The King's Royal Bestiary*?"

"With all due respect, Your Majesty, I don't think such a book should exist."

Stonehorn's face was one of surprise. "But the truth. The stories . . ."

". . . are not mine to tell," said Kenny. "And the truth is . . . complicated."

"I would agree, sire," added Flit. "A single book simply cannot hold all the facts learned in a lifetime. However, perhaps some of these fabulous creatures

will go on to share their stories for us all to enjoy."

"Now, that is a splendid idea," said Grahame.

"Then let it be so," said Stonehorn. "I do look forward to expanding the library with new stories. In the meantime, Master Kenny, I have something for you."

He led Kenny, his family, and his friends to the roundabout at the castle's entrance. There, a footman came forth bearing a wooden box. He bowed and handed it to the king.

"George tells me your beloved automobile perished in your effort to liberate those that Nesbit had entrapped." Stonehorn opened the box and handed a booklet to Kenny. It was the owner's manual to a Jolt Silver Phantom.

"Your . . . Your Majesty . . . this is for your car" was all Kenny could sputter out.

"Not my car, yours." The king handed him the keys. "Besides, I never could get the hang of these crazy machines." He leaned close. "And I know you youngsters love zipping around in them."

On cue, two cars raced up the castle's cobble-stone drive.

"Hey!" the king yelled at his sons. "What did I

tell you? Slow down! And stay off the royal lawn!"
He chased after his children.

Kenny caught his father stroking the shiny
silver fender of the car. "What do ya think of this
automobile, Pa?"

"I don' think you'll have any blast-plosions
with this one," his father replied with a wink.

Kenny's mother rushed up and squeezed him
tight. "I am so proud of you," she said, and kissed
his forehead. A footman loaded Kenny's sisters

onto a royal carriage for their return trip home. His parents climbed aboard and waved as the carriage rolled down the drive. "We'll see ya back home, Kit," his father called back. Kenny was joined by his friends as he bid them farewell.

"Well, now you'll be able to visit anytime you like." George gestured to the car.

"Yes, please come see us soon." Flit shook Kenny's paw vigorously. "You are always welcome."

"I will take you up on that offer, I promise," replied Kenny. He patted George on the back. "Let's keep our chess game going. We can send each other our moves via postcard."

"I like the sound of that, my squire," replied George. A broad smile shone behind his bushy mustache.

Kenny opened the door to his new car, and Charlotte slipped into the passenger seat. Porky and Polly piled in behind while he turned the crank and started the engine. "You ready, Grahame?" he asked as he climbed behind the wheel.

"I think I'm gonna stay a spell." Grahame watched a pair of griffins fly around the castle tower. "You know, help the newbies get adjusted to royal life. I can bring them up to date on food trends, the latest fashions . . . that sort of thing."

"Ooo! An Ambassador of Arcane Spirits," said Flit.

"Now, I like the sound of that," replied Dante. The rescued manticore cub at his side nodded in agreement.

Kenny put on a brave face in light of Grahame's announcement. He knew with his head that his friend was doing the right thing, but in his heart he'd miss him. "Well, I certainly have many souvenirs from this adventure."

"So do I, my friend." The dragon and rabbit embraced.

"Don't worry," said Dante. "We'll all be sick of crème brûlée soon enough."

Kenny laughed, despite the sadness he felt. "I'll see you soon, then."

"I'll see you soon," replied Grahame.

Kenny started up the car. He turned to look at Grahame once more as the car rolled away.

"Goodbye," he whispered.

And So . . .

Kenny returned to his life on Rabbit Farm, where he went to school, did his chores, and even babysat his sisters. He filled the rest of his time reading and managing his bookstore. You see, his mother kept the gift that George had given him, and, of course, Kenny accepted it. The Burrow Bookshop reopened under new management, featuring a little café selling freshly baked goods, courtesy of Old Rabbit Farm.

It seemed like whenever Kenny felt the pang of missing one of his friends, a letter would arrive recounting the latest news and gossip, or Kenny would

And So . . .

write about his own life. More than ever, he looked forward to Charlotte's sparkly smile and laughter while spending time with her at work or on the weekend playing board games. He even bought fifteen tickets for the performance of The Taming of the Shrew *and brought his entire family. They stood and cheered when Charlotte was called onstage for her elaborate costumes.*

Kenny's father burst into the kitchen one winter evening, his eyes as wide as saucers. "You're not gonna—"

"Hey, Old Man Winter." Kenny's mother cut him off. She pointed at him with a ladle. "Take those snow-covered shoes and coat off. I don't want your melted puddles all over my clean kitchen floor."

"But, Ma," he whimpered.

"I know you're all riled up, but you can talk and take your shoes off at the same time." She returned to her cooking.

"What is it, Papa?" asked Katy as she ground pepper into the broth her mother was cooking.

"Tell us," the others asked.

And So . . .

"First, where's Kit?" their father responded.

"Right here, Pa," said Kenny, holding a stack of bowls. George and Flit were placing them around the kitchen table. All three were dressed in identical tacky sweaters—a homemade holiday gift from Charlotte.

"You're not gonna believe what I saw up on ol' Shepard's Hill." His father pointed out the kitchen window.

Kenny set the stack of bowls down. "No! Are you serious?"

"As a hungry horsefly."

"Pa, why didn't you say so?" said Kenny's mother.

His father looked over at her, then did a double take, but Kenny didn't see it. He was already out the door.

"Coats and hats, Kenny!" his mother called after him. "You're not setting a good example for your sisters."

———✦———

Kenny led his family and friends up the sloping hill just as the last rays of the sun lit the winter sky in shades of pink and purple. The powdery snow muffled their footsteps as they trudged toward the amphitheater. Above them, countless stars winked awake and filled the horizon with dazzling radiance. A large silhouette glided over the family and landed at the top of the cave while smoke rose in little puffs from within.

Kenny lit his lantern and held it high as he approached. A pair of griffins perched on the top of the cave smiled down at him, while a hippogriff settled under a nearby tree for the night. A small herd of unicorns cavorted around the family in the drifts of snow, sending up plumes of shimmering flakes.

The golden glow within the cave illuminated the familiar shape of a round, scruffy dragon. His lemony eyes twinkled in the dark, and his toothy grin spread from ear to ear.

Kenny could feel the warmth of tears on his cheeks as he rushed toward the cave.

"Hello."